DIVING FOR PEARLS

The Complete Collection

MELISSA STORM

ISBN: 978-1-942771-29-6

Editor:

Stevie Mikayne

Cover and Interior Design:

Mallory Rock

Proofreader:

Mary Metcalfe

PO Box 721
Union Lake, MI 48387

To anyone who needs to be reminded that angels watch over us, and to Phoenix, my darling daughter, the one who at last made me believe.

AUTHOR'S PREFACE

How can I even begin to convey how personal and deeply meaningful this story is for me? Perhaps I'll start with the true story that inspired it.

In 2013, I was heavily pregnant, expecting my first child and facing a number of complications, both physical and emotional. The preeclampsia, polyhydraminos, and sciatica all severely limited my activity, but the onset of pregnancy-induced Obsessive Compulsive Disorder kept my mind spinning all hours of the night, wondering *what if?*—always picturing the grimmest of possible outcomes for me and my child.

Then one day, all my fears came to a head. I was admitted to the hospital after an abnormal ultrasound and was told I couldn't leave without first having a cesarean section and bringing my baby into the world. All my fears of the past several months converged, and I was convinced I would die, had prepared myself for the end.

Only, instead of greeting death, I said hello to the most precious little girl, thus beginning a new, better life. I felt instantly better once I was no longer weighed down by the 11 ½ lb child in my womb, but I also couldn't forget the months of fear.

Every day felt like a blessing, having survived the unsurvivable, and I began to wonder *what if?*—once again, crying tears of joy for being able to accompany my daughter through her life. But I also knew my love for her was so strong that we'd still find a way to be together even if I hadn't made it out of the operating room with my life intact.

That's when I met Elizabeth. Her story starts where a new chapter of mine also turned the page: on the operating table and with eclampsia. While I pulled through, she didn't—but fate provided a way for her to be there to help her daughter through life regardless.

This story, which started as a thought exercise, quickly became a love letter to my daughter, and evolved even further to encompass my answers to all of life's most difficult questions.

What is the meaning of life?

Why do bad things happen to good people?

Is Heaven real? What is it like? What about Hell?

Are angels among us?

Elizabeth's story provides my answers, answers that have given me peace as I face each new obstacle in life, as I watch my baby grow into a young lady, as I continue to strive to live life to its fullest, and just to be.

This journey wasn't just Elizabeth's—but mine also—and I hope you'll find a special place in your heart for it too.

Happy reading,

Melissa S.

"Love is life. All, everything that I understand, I understand only because I love. Everything is, everything exists, only because I love. Everything is united by it alone. Love is God, and to die means that I, a particle of love, shall return to the general and eternal source."

Leo Tolstoy

PART I

A strange pressing sensation, that's how it started. Elizabeth moved her hand away from her full, pregnant belly, but still the phantom pushing feeling continued, even stronger than before.

"Theo..." She shook her husband awake. "I think it may be time."

Theo slung an arm across her torso and mumbled without even bothering to open his eyes.

Pain shot from her bellybutton down into her legs, twisting as it crawled toward her toes. She let out a gasp and wrapped her arms around herself to try to keep from screaming.

Theo shot upright, an expression of concern tugging at his worn features. "How can it be time? The due date is more than a month away. It's too early."

Elizabeth nodded. Tears fell onto her pajama bottoms, splashing the happy, pink clouds.

"Okay, okay. Let's go. Everything is going to be okay, honey. It's gotta be."

She let him pull her to her feet and usher her to the car parked outside on the curb, but somehow Elizabeth couldn't believe her husband's promise, no matter how much she wanted to.

"Eclampsia," the doctor said with a frown. He stood at the end of Elizabeth's bed and studied her chart.

A million thoughts raced through Elizabeth's mind, but the only one that mattered was *will my baby be okay?* She bit her lower lip to keep the tears at bay. If she was going to get through this, she'd need to be strong.

"We'll take good care of you." A nurse smiled as she pushed an IV into the back of Elizabeth's hand. "Everything will be all right."

"The baby has to come out now. The OR is just finishing up with the last cesarean. As soon as they're done sanitizing the room, you'll be headed in. I need to go help them get ready, but I will see you again soon." The doctor dashed out, even though there was so much Elizabeth needed to ask. Everything was moving at the speed of light, too fast to contemplate. This definitely wasn't the birth plan she'd envisioned.

"Smile. You're going to meet your baby today." The nurse squeezed Elizabeth's hand.

Minutes later they wheeled her into a sterile room engulfed in white and metal. It looked more mental ward than maternity. Theo had been made to wait out in the hall. They'd pushed throw-away scrubs and a hospital mask his way, told him to change, said he could join her once they had begun. But she needed him now, needed him to whisper jokes in her ear as the anesthetist shoved a long needle into her spine, needed him as they moved her from the gurney to the operating table, as they put up the curtain and sliced into her abdomen.

And she knew even before the monitor beside her started beeping wildly out of control, even before someone shouted "BP's 240 over 160 and climbing fast" and several other someones hovered above her, injecting things into her arms, pressing other things into her chest, speaking loudly and moving swiftly.

Please let my baby be okay, she prayed even though the words couldn't find her lips. And the last thing she heard before it all faded to static was the sound of her newborn taking that precious first breath and crying into the chaos that surrounded them.

Everything went white.

The unyielding wall of white surrounded her like an embrace, absorbed her, became her. Nothing existed except for the vast blankness. She drifted through it, a mere ripple in the endless ocean. Time passed, but not in any discernible way. She didn't know where she was or why, but she also didn't think to question this new plane of existence. It, like she, just *was.*

The milky infinity at last separated to reveal the silhouette of an enormous city on the horizon. And this city was made of all the most spectacular colors in the sky's repertoire—pinks, purples, oranges, yellows, blue—an impossibly beautiful structure built of sunrise. Flanking the ethereal village stood two soaring gates made of the finest yellow gold and dotted with pearls, each of which loomed larger than the distant moon.

The current carried her forward, but before she could pass through the gates, a figure materialized to bar her entrance.

"Elizabeth," it said, and at once she remembered who she was and how she had come here.

I died—the acknowledgment flooded her awareness, but it did not make her sad. Her body now formed around her, but it felt clunky and foreign.

"I am Peter," the man said as his body also materialized before her—a dimpled chin, wavy blond hair, and long limbs. The perfect likeness of someone she knew very well. *Theo.*

"You look exactly like my husband, but how?"

"I made myself familiar to give you comfort, for we have much to discuss."

"Am I in Heaven?" she asked, already sure of the answer.

"Yes. Do you remember how you died?"

Elizabeth thought back to her last moments on Earth. A cry escaped before she could choke it back. "Please tell me, Peter—is my baby okay?"

"Yes, she is. Your sacrifice saved her."

Her? I had a girl? Tears of joy sprang to her eyes. As magnificent as her new home had proven, she also couldn't bear the thought of never knowing her daughter, of leaving her baby without a mother, leaving her husband without a partner.

Peter placed a hand on her shoulder, and although she couldn't feel it, the gesture still brought comfort. He waited until her racing thoughts slowed, waited for her to work her situation out, and continue their conversation.

"So is this it? Do I cross through those gates, and never see my family again?" She raised both arms to motion toward the gates—so tall they appeared to carry on forever into the sky.

"Your life is over, yes, but this is not the end of your journey. You are not ready for Heaven, Elizabeth."

Fear took hold as she murmured, "Are you sending me to that other place?"

Peter chortled. "No, no, not at all. But, you see, you aren't yet ready to cross through those gates and become a Pearl. Your heart is still tied to the world. To live here, your heart must be free and ready for paradise."

"I... I don't understand."

"You've proven your capacity for great love by sacrificing yourself in order to save your daughter. You also miss her and need her in the same way she will need your protection as she goes through life. While I cannot undo what has already been done, I can send you back to Earth. You will be transformed into a special kind of angel, a protector."

"You're making me a guardian angel?"

"Yes, so you can watch over your daughter and know your sacrifice was not in vain, so you will complete your unfinished business, and so that you will be ready. Come with me. I will make everything clear."

Elizabeth blinked, and when she opened her eyes again, she found herself in the hospital room from before. The scents of hand sanitizer and baby formula mingled in the air, saturating her consciousness. Across the room, a stooped figure hunched over in a chair crying softly.

Theo, the real Theo. She rushed to his side and reached for his hand to give it a squeeze. But her fingers passed right through his.

"Remember, you don't have a body anymore. It will take some getting used to." She turned to face the angel, taking in his tall, lanky frame and dark features. He no longer held Theo's form.

"But I can see. I can hear. I can smell. How am I able to do all that without a body?" She tried once again to caress her husband. He was so close but so unattainable—pure torture.

"You have the senses you need to do your job. Nothing more." Peter's expression was solemn as if he had chosen to hold back something important. Elizabeth was just about to ask for clarification, when a petite nurse entered the room pushing a large cart in ahead of her.

"Somebody wants to see her daddy." The nurse's peppy voice did not match her worn expression.

Theo raised his head and wiped the backs of his hands across his face. "I don't know if I'm ready..."

"Ready or not, this baby needs you. You're all she's got now." The nurse gave him an apologetic tilt of the head and pressed the baby into his arms.

"But that's not true," Elizabeth argued. "I'm right here. She has me. Theo, you have me."

Theo stared straight ahead, seemingly unable to glance down at the child who had so recently replaced his wife as the number one person in his life.

"Honey, it's okay. You can love her. You need to love her. For me," Elizabeth pleaded while Peter steepled his fingers in front of his chest.

Theo sniffled and ventured a glance toward the pink bundle that squirmed in his lap.

"That's it," Peter whispered. "Keep talking to him."

She took a deep breath and then told Theo that she was here, that she loved them both so much, that everything was going to be all right. By the time she had finished what she needed to say, a smile had overtaken her husband's sullen expression.

He bent down to kiss the baby's forehead. "It's just you and me now, baby. You and me against the world."

The baby cooed and suckled on her receiving blanket, and Theo chuckled softly.

"But I can't call you baby forever, can I? You need a name."

Elizabeth bent over Theo's shoulder to look her newborn in the face. "Please name her Daisy," she whispered. "I always wanted a little girl named Daisy."

Theo perked up as if he'd heard her simple plea. A moment later Elizabeth's suspicion was confirmed when he lifted the baby toward his face and said, "You know what? I think I'll call you *Daisy*."

As soon as the words escaped Theo's mouth, the scene around Elizabeth began to dissolve.

After a brief journey through the incredible whiteness, Elizabeth once again found herself standing next to Peter outside of the gates to Heaven. His true form was still a shock to her.

"Why did you bring us back here? I thought I wasn't ready for Heaven yet?"

"That's true, but before you can officially begin your duties, you need to learn what's allowed and what isn't allowed. You need to know the rules." Peter paced back and forth before the gates. "First of all, there are four types of beings. There's God, then there are angels like me and like you now too. We also have humans and Pearls."

"Pearls? I've never heard of that before."

"Pearls are the luckiest beings there are. They are the people who have completed their earthly journeys and are able to retire forever beyond those gates. They live side by side with God in perfect bliss." Peter gave a wistful sigh and fixed his eyes on his charge.

"What about angels? Don't you—I mean, we—get to be in Heaven too?"

"We are separate, eternal servants. It is our job to help humans fulfill their potential. Most of us never get the chance to cross over."

"Most, but not all?" She drummed a finger against her lips as she waited for Peter to explain.

"Not you, Elizabeth. Protector angels are special. Once their charges achieve their potential, the protectors are invited to join them where they too become Pearls."

"So what you're saying... One day Daisy and I will enter Heaven together?" her voice cracked as emotion swept over her.

"That's exactly what I'm saying."

"And Theo?"

"Has his own protector. You will see him again on the other side when you are both ready."

"So when they die, we'll all be together again? Just like Nana always told me growing up."

"N-n-no, that's not exactly accurate," Peter stuttered. "There's no guarantee one life will be enough."

Elizabeth's eyes crossed as she attempted to make sense of that.

"Most people need tens, even hundreds, of lifetimes to get it right. Very few are able to transcend after their first attempt."

"Are you talking about reincarnation?" Elizabeth asked.

Peter nodded. "That's one word for it, yes."

A tremor worked its way through her body, but Elizabeth pressed on. "So if Daisy doesn't make it to Heaven this time, will she go to Hell? Will she be born again?"

"Hell is not a place you need to worry about. In fact, it's not a *place* at all. And with you at her side, Daisy will do well. I'm sure of it."

While Elizabeth wanted to know more about Hell, she was far more interested in learning about how she could fulfill her guardian angel obligations and give her daughter the best possible life. She waited for Peter to continue.

"If Daisy isn't ready after this lifetime, she will be born again, yes. And you will stay with her as many times as it takes for her to be ready."

"Even if she's not my daughter anymore?"

Peter closed the distance between them and stopped just inches from her face. He fixed his gaze on her and said, "You aren't her mother anymore, but what you are is so much more special than that. There is no closer bond in existence than that of a protector and her charge. When you and Daisy at last get to meet inside those gates, it will be as if you are two halves finally merging into a whole. You will have the perfect friendship for all of eternity. There is no greater gift that anyone could receive."

Elizabeth was sure she spied a tear welling up behind Peter's eyes, but he turned away quickly and redirected their conversation.

"Do you have any questions?"

"I don't think—"

"Then it is time." Peter's snap transported them back to her old house.

Night enveloped the room, yet Elizabeth had no trouble making out the tiny form in the bassinet—the baby's chest rising and falling in perfect syncopation to her father's soft snores.

"Call if you need me," Peter instructed before disappearing from sight.

Elizabeth stood in place. This was the first moment in the rest of her eternity, and she wanted to get it perfect. She padded over to the edge of the lace-trimmed bassinet and leaned forward, sucking in the sweet scent of her little girl.

"Mommy loves you, little baby," she sang, trailing immaterial fingers over Daisy's rosy cheek.

The baby's eyes opened at her touch, and a smile lit her small face.

An enormous sense of love took over Elizabeth's entire being. She understood exactly what Peter had meant when he called Daisy her soulmate. And she knew right then that an eternity could never be long enough.

PART II

Elizabeth stretched an immaterial hand toward her late husband, but knowing she couldn't touch him sent a fresh torrent of tears down her cheeks. Daisy's cry sounded through the monitor, and Elizabeth felt a tug toward the nursery. She loved her daughter—wanted to go to her—but she hated that she could do nothing to lessen her husband's pain; hated that he was so close but still impossibly out of reach.

Elizabeth drifted into the baby's room, and she immediately stopped crying. A smile spread from one chubby cheek to the next.

"Hi, sweetie. Mommy's here now."

Daisy cooed and kicked her tiny legs.

"Can you… Can you see me?" Elizabeth floated from one end of the crib to the other, and the baby's eyes trailed after her.

"You can. Can't you? But how?"

The baby smiled again as Elizabeth drew closer.

"Yes, Mommy's here. Mommy will always be here for you, little one."

Theo let out a low, guttural moan from the other room and began muttering to himself. "Why? Why? Why did you have to take her from me? Why?" He stared up toward the ceiling fan, as if he could look his maker straight in the face and demand an answer.

"I'm here, Theo. Right here for you," she answered, but he didn't turn to look at her like their daughter had.

Instead, he picked up the bottle of Xanax the therapist had given him and shook several of the potent little pills into his palm.

"I could end it right now, you know. What's the point anyway?" He lifted the handful of poison to his mouth, but then Daisy cried again.

Theo hesitated for a second before dropping the pills on his nightstand and tromping into the nursery—his face red and raw. But Daisy smiled, happy to see her daddy.

"She needs you, Theo. Please don't abandon our little girl," Elizabeth urged.

And whether or not he heard her, Theo reached into the crib and raised the infant to his chest, clutching her tightly as if he were afraid that letting go of her would mean letting go of everything.

Once Elizabeth was sure the danger had passed, she stepped out into the sunlight and called to Peter. At once, the wrangler angel appeared, using his favorite tall, dark, and lanky form.

"Yes, Elizabeth," he stated flatly.

"You said to call if I needed anything."

"Yes." His expression remained cool and unchanged, but Elizabeth continued, hoping the desperation in her voice would break through his tough exterior.

"Theo. He's so sad. I need to help."

"Theo isn't your charge. Daisy is."

"I just—"

"Theo has his own protector to watch over him." Peter crossed his arms over his chest and shifted his nonexistent weight from one foot to the next. Elizabeth always found it funny how she and the other angels kept these physical gestures long after separating from their bodies.

"But where? I'm the only one here."

"That's not so. Daniel is near."

"Daniel? But I haven't seen anyone for days. Even the family isn't coming by to check on Theo anymore."

"Daniel is near," Peter repeated. "You just can't see him."

"Like Theo can't see me."

"Correct."

"But Daisy can?"

"Also correct." Peter peeked at Elizabeth over his shoulder as he walked toward the large oak tree in their front yard.

Elizabeth followed, stumbling after him. She hated moving through walls, but she had no way to open doors and she didn't want Peter to leave without helping her. "Why can she see me, and why can't Theo? And where is Daniel?"

"So many questions." Peter shook his head. "We'll take one at a time. First, Daisy can see you, because babies are close to the Gates. They're not fully integrated in the mortal realm, so they can interact with ours as well."

"And Theo?"

"Is fully integrated and won't be able to see or hear you, no matter what you do."

"But Daniel. Why can't I see him? Isn't he an angel like us?"

"Like you, yes. But protectors aren't supposed to worry about anyone or anything other than their charges. Yours is Daisy, not Theo." He sighed. "You need to stop paying so much attention to him. You're doing a disservice to Daisy with this obsession."

"But he was my husband."

"He's not anymore. And you're not technically Daisy's mother either. You're her protector, which is so much more."

Elizabeth whipped around in front of Peter and stood close to him. "If I can't help Theo, then I'll need to speak to someone who can. Take me to Daniel. "

"How many times must I explain? You're here for Daisy."

She huffed. "And if Daisy's father kills himself, then what? Seems I need to protect him in order to keep her safe too."

Peter frowned and looked toward the sky. "Well, you may have a point there. Fine." He snapped and disappeared, leaving a frail-looking angel in his wake.

She turned toward the red-headed youth with freckles splashed across his rather large nose. "Are you Daniel?" she asked.

"Yup."

"Hi, I'm Elizabeth." She extended her hand, but Daniel just laughed.

"I know. I used to watch you all the time when you were on the other side." His cheeks crimsoned, and he looked toward the ground.

She decided not to ask about when and how he was watching her then. Besides, his flushed expression already said more than she cared to know.

"We have to help Theo," she insisted, hoping Daniel would prove more reasonable than Peter.

"Believe me, I'm trying, lady. Really, I am."

"Okay, then tell me how I can help."

"Well, basically, you can't. I'm his protector, see?" Daniel squinted up at her, his gaze somehow both intimidating and meek.

"We can't let him kill himself."

"Sometimes it's all part of the plan. We can't interfere with the plan."

She raised her voice. If she couldn't appeal to the angel's kindness, maybe she could get him to cooperate in some other way. "Is it part of the plan for Theo to commit suicide and leave little Daisy an orphan?"

"God, no! I was just saying. You know, hypothetically."

"So if it's not in the plan, then he can't kill himself, right?"

"Well, I didn't say that..."

"Then how could you just stand back and watch him suffer like this? Why aren't you doing your job?"

He jabbed a finger at her, a sudden rage twisted his features. "Hey, I do what I can! Besides you're a rookie. I bet you don't even know the first thing about what we can and can't do anyway."

"Show me."

His features softened as he looked her over. "What?"

"I want to learn."

Daniel let out a low moan. "Ugh, this is supposed to be Peter's job. What good is he if he can't even show the newbs the ropes without a little help from old Daniel?"

Elizabeth laughed despite herself. "Old? You couldn't be more than nine years old."

"I may have been young when I died, but I've been around the block with these here wings more times than I bet you can count."

"Sounds like there's a lot you could teach me then. Would you? Please?"

Daniel cricked his neck to either side and then cracked his knuckles. "I suppose I can help the lady out. First, you gotta learn how to whisper."

Elizabeth raised her hand to speak, but he cut her off before she could say anything.

"Not whispering, *whispering*, if you know what I mean. You know that still small voice mortals hear telling them to do what's right? You think they come up with that on their own? No! That's us. That's *the whisper*. You lean forward like this and put your face right into their brain. Don't worry, they can't feel it and you can't see it. Thank God you can't see it. But you gotta get real close to be heard, see? So you lean into their brains, and then you say your piece. That's the most important tool at our disposal."

"Whisper. Got it. What else?"

"The other really good thing to know is the dodge. You know, like dodgeball. You see them red rubber things flying your way and—BAM!—you fly to this side, that side, whichever side to avoid getting hit right in the kisser."

Elizabeth nodded. "The dodge. How do I do that?"

"No, you don't do it. You get them to do it, right? So to dodge, you gotta lean into them again, and then you push or pull, whichever way, to get them to move.

It's just like how they call the whisper their conscience. They call this one muscle memory. Muscle memory, my hiney. That's all us."

"I thought muscle memory was how people remember to ride a bike or play the piano, things like that."

"Yeah, we do that too if we get bored enough. But our number one job is as a protector, not a muse. Besides, with a baby, you'll have plenty to keep you busy."

"Okay. The whisper and the dodge. Is that it?"

"What do you mean *is that it*? That gives you power over their thoughts and their bodies. What more do you need, huh? Oh, but one last thing. Don't go messing with Theo. He's mine, and I tend to get a little protective."

And just as quickly as he had appeared in the first place, Daniel was gone.

Elizabeth kept close watch over Daisy, but was unable to let her attachment to Theo go. Occasionally, Daniel would show up to chastise her, but mostly she found herself alone with her thoughts. Eternity felt like a very long time, having no one to spend it with.

She tried both the whisper and the dodge out on Daisy, but neither accomplished much. After all, the baby couldn't even walk or speak yet, which made it all the more difficult to trust Theo to Daniel.

Still, the days wore on, and Theo wore on right along with them. And while he still seemed sullen, he no longer studied the pill bottle like it held the cure for all his worries. With time, he even started putting on his jeans again, then he started shaving, then heading out to run errands, and finally—when she'd been gone from his realm for months—she heard a deep laugh erupt from Theo's chest.

"Now that's my girl," he crooned as he swung the baby around in his arms and they continued to chuckle together. When he set Daisy down upon her feet, the baby took first one tentative step forward and then another.

"Oh, Theo!" Elizabeth cried. "Our little girl is growing up so fast." And she was. In fact, it seemed like only yesterday Elizabeth had…

No, she didn't want to go there. It was much easier to do her job as a protector if she pushed aside the nagging reminder that she could only fulfill this role because she wasn't able to serve in her rightful roles on Earth.

She choked back the very mortal emotions of loss and regret. Like Daisy, she too was on the cusp of both worlds. How long would it be until she lost her human longing? And did she want to lose the last part of her that made her who she'd been, who she still was?

Life, as always, was a mystery, and unfortunately not even death provided an answer. Maybe when she and Daisy crossed through the Gates, maybe then she'd have all the answers she'd ever sought and many more besides.

Theo left to grab his camera, providing Daisy with the perfect opportunity to make mischief, and Elizabeth her first real opportunity to try the dodge.

The little girl toddled toward the end table and reached for the hot mug of coffee Theo had left unattended.

Elizabeth shot forward, pushing herself into Daisy and swinging her arms wildly to the side. It worked.

Daisy fell forward in a clumsy spin and crumpled into a heap on the floor. She looked right at Elizabeth and let out the most pitiful cry. This would be the first of many times, Elizabeth realized, she'd have to hurt her daughter in order to help her.

Theo rushed in and picked the little girl up into his strong arms. Elizabeth wished there was still a place in those arms for her too. Missing him never got any easier, and she doubted it ever would—on this side of the Gates or otherwise.

Everything changed once Daisy started walking. Now Elizabeth needed to keep constant watch over her to redirect those tiny hands and feet and keep them away from danger. The flurry of activity was good for Theo too. He chased after Daisy all hours of the day and night, leaving him too exhausted to do anything but sleep at the end of each day.

More so than ever before, they were united in their individual quests to keep their daughter safe. But as she felt her bonds to Theo strengthening, she'd noticed that Daisy had begun to fade away. Or rather, she herself had begun to fade.

Sure, she could still dodge and she found the occasional opportunity to whisper, but she could no longer grab Daisy's attention with words and gestures.

"She's anchoring," Peter said when she called to him for help. "I fear it won't be long now. But don't worry. It means you've done your job well. It means she's growing, and so are you. Besides, you'll have plenty to keep you busy as she discovers the world and all the many opportunities for danger and sin. Now go with them." Peter gestured toward Theo who was zipping up Daisy's pink jacket while balancing the oversized diaper bag on his shoulder.

"Ready to go to the park?" he asked, straightening the lopsided bow affixed to Daisy's curls.

"Yes, Daddy!" Daisy mumbled then burst into giggles. They were off.

Elizabeth never knew what to do with herself while Daisy and Theo were in the car. It felt strange to sit when she had no material form, and it felt equally uncomfortable to float along beside the vehicle while other cars passed through her on the road. Today, she chose to float a few inches above the car in order to keep an eye on Daisy with minimal pass-throughs.

When they arrived, she found Daniel standing near the swings at the park. "The swings were my favorite when I was—well, when I was alive."

"Mine too," she confided, shooting a sympathetic look his way. While she wondered about the story behind the nine-year-old angel, she didn't want to bring any of his painful longing to the surface. Just as she wouldn't want anyone to remind her of what she'd lost—that is, if she actually ever found a way to move past it.

"I'm on a mission today, and you won't like it. But what can I say? It's the plan. And you know we can't mess with the plan."

Elizabeth gulped and fixed her gaze on Daisy as the child flew down the slide and into her daddy's arms.

"It's time." Daniel's expression was happy, though his words were grim.

"Time for what?" she nudged.

"Time for Theo and Daisy to move on past… well, past you."

Elizabeth opened her mouth to argue, but no words came out. What could she say to change the angel's mind? Even if she could find the right argument, she knew it was selfish to expect Theo to remain committed to her memory and without a partner in life.

Daniel came over to pat her on the shoulder. "There, there now. We both knew this couldn't last forever. Besides, it's what's right for him. You do love him, don't you?"

"Of course, I do."

"Then let him be free. Let him move on from the grief of losing you by finding somebody else." He paused for a moment and smiled, raising his hand to point out into the parking lot. "Look, there she is now."

Elizabeth watched as a petite, dark-skinned woman approached, holding firmly to the leash for a tiny hound.

"Her name is Tina," Daniel supplied. "She lost somebody important too. That's what's going to unite them, as a matter of fact. And that's Mitzi." He pointed to the Daschund at Tina's feet. "This is her last visit to the park. Tina's putting her down afterward. The cancer's gone too far, you see. It's causing them both too much pain."

Elizabeth didn't know what to say, so she remained silent as she watched the scene unfold.

Daisy ran up to the little dog and gave her a big hug around the neck. "Puppy!" she cried, then giggled as Mitzi gave her kisses on the face.

"Daisy!" Theo called, running after her. He saw Tina standing there and blushed. "I'm sorry. She just loves dogs. C'mon, Daze. Let's go back to the slide."

"No, that's okay," Tina said before Theo could turn away. "I don't mind. It's nice actually. My name's Tina, and this is Mitzi. She always did love children." Tina sucked back a tear, and Theo placed a hand on her wrist.

"Is everything okay?" His eyes searched hers, much the way they had searched Elizabeth's as she woke him up that fateful night to tell her Daisy was on the way.

Tina grinned and took a seat on the bench. Theo sat beside her as the two littles played with each other in the grass.

"Do you mind if we not talk about that? I could use a friend right now, and a distraction."

"Sure."

"Your little girl is so sweet. I bet she gets that from her mother."

Theo looked down at his empty hands and sighed. "She does. It's a shame Daisy never got to know her."

Elizabeth sucked in a deep breath. She'd cry if she still could with her immaterial body.

"You know, it's for the best." Daniel stood beside her, watching over the budding friendship. "Theo needs a partner, and Daisy needs a mother."

"But I just miss them both so much. I didn't want to say goodbye, and I don't think I'm ready now either."

"You are ready. The plan is perfect. You shouldn't question it."

"But I feel like I'm losing them both all over again. Theo to her." She nodded toward Tina. "And Daisy because I'm fading out of her life."

"Don't think like that, lady. Jeez. Now you're making *me* sad." He sniffed and rubbed his face into his sleeve.

"But she can't see me like she used to."

"She can feel you, and in a lot of ways that's better."

Elizabeth looked toward the paved walkway, trying to push her emotions back down. "I guess. I just wish I could've waved goodbye first. Wish that I'd had some kind of warning."

Daniel leaned forward into her line of vision and smiled. "Say goodbye now. It'll help, I promise."

"Oh, what could it hurt?" She stepped forward into the neatly cut grass and waved to her daughter. "Daisy, I want to say goodbye, baby, but it doesn't mean I'm going anywhere. I will always be right here for you."

The little girl glanced up, her eyes fixed directly on her protector.

"Look, Daddy!" She pointed at Elizabeth and giggled. "A butterfly."

PART III

White flowers hung down from an overhead trellis and gossamer fabric fluttered in the soft breeze, giving the normally urbane backyard an ethereal feel. Tina appeared, stunning in her classic A-line gown, embroidered with delicate, pink pearls.

Elizabeth couldn't shake the sad sense of nostalgia, not on this day, because it should have been her. It *had been* her a lifetime ago, and now...

She floated toward her late husband, allowing herself to pretend if only just for a moment.

Theo's face had aged so much in the time since Elizabeth had moved toward the Gates, yet he remained as handsome as ever. His eyes bore straight through her and fixed on his new bride as she made her ascent to the altar. Although Elizabeth hated to admit it, Tina did look lovely. Her dark complexion contrasted beautifully with the form-fitting, ivory gown. Her black eyes beamed as she walked toward her future husband.

Then there was Daisy, a vision in pink, her bouncing curls spritzed to perfection. She giggled as she held onto the leash of her fluffy Pomeranian puppy—so proud to be standing there with her daddy as they added this new member to the family.

Tina was the only mother she'd ever known, Elizabeth realized yet again, a deep sense of loss settling into the pit of her nonexistent stomach.

She'd known today was coming, known for a long time, but that didn't make the actual occasion any easier. Sure, she was glad that Theo had found happiness once again, that Daisy had one more person to love and look out for her. But the already strained ties to her earthly life frayed even further, now that a replacement had been brought in.

"It's the plan," the other angels told her. "Don't question the plan." But she questioned it anyway. What made Tina worthy of living the life that had been ripped away from her? And why had Elizabeth been forced to watch from the sidelines as a "reward" for her sacrifice in saving her baby's life?

Now they were slipping rings onto each other's fingers and saying "I will" instead of the more traditional "I do". Daisy even got to participate by allowing Tina to slip a two-tone gold and silver Claddagh ring onto her tiny finger.

She held tight onto Daisy's hands even after placing the ring and said, "Daisy, I love you every bit as much as I love your father, and I'm so excited to be your new mommy. I know I can't replace the mother you lost, and I wouldn't want to, but I also want you to know that even though you didn't come from my belly, you have my full heart. I will be mother and friend, and I will cherish my role in this new family we are building together." She squeezed Daisy's hands and let go, then both bride and groom bent down to kiss the little girl on her rosy cheeks, sharing their first kiss not as man and wife, but as a family—a whole, perfect family.

They had no idea that family included an angel, who floated nearby wiping tears away from her cheeks with the backs of her hands. Nor did they have any idea how much their happiness both fulfilled and broke her.

After the reception, a shiny black limo spirited Theo and Tina away. Daisy was left with her grandma and her brand new puppy to keep her company during the couple's honeymoon in Belize.

"Want to go rent a movie from the grocery store?" Nana asked, pulling her oversized bag onto her shoulder and sliding her feet into a worn pair of clogs. "We can get the fixings for some Toll House cookies while we're there too."

Poor Nana always tried so hard.

Daisy looked up from her game of tug with the puppy she'd merrily dubbed Cricket. "Can we get sprinkles for the cookies too?" She pushed a stray bit of bang from her eyes.

Nana, of course, said "yes," and the two were off.

When they reached the supermarket, Nana deposited Daisy in front of the Redbox machine. "Pick something good for us while I gather what we need for our little baking adventure." And just like that, she was off, leaving the six-year-old to herself with the coloring movie vending machine.

Elizabeth shook her head. Nana tried so hard to be Daisy's friend, that she often forgot how to be her protector. Luckily, Elizabeth was always hovering nearby, fully devoted to this necessary job.

Seemingly unfazed by the novelty of being alone in public, the little girl thumbed through the carousel of options and immediately decided on the newest Disney princess movie—the one both she and Nana had already seen half a dozen times—then she wandered over to look at the prizes stuffed inside the claw machine.

After that, she found her way over to the dizzying array of candies spread out before a nearby checkout line. This was one of the many lanes that were currently closed to customers, which meant no one was manning the aisle. Daisy realized this too and filched a bag of Reese's Pieces, sticking them into the waistband of her purple jeans.

Elizabeth was so shocked by the whole thing, she almost forgot that she had a job to do. After all, her most important role was as her daughter's conscience. As Daisy continued to browse the selection of candy, Elizabeth leaned forward, pushing her ghostly face into the little girl's head. Next came the whisper.

This isn't right. Just because no one's watching doesn't mean the candy is free. You should put it back. Besides, Nana is making cookies. With sprinkles.

Elizabeth snapped back and watched as Daisy fished the candy packet from her pants and put it back into the display, then skipped back over to the Redbox machine to wait for her nana.

Pop. Poof.

Elizabeth heard their laughter before their forms actually materialized.

"Good job, newbie." Daniel's face was red with laughter. "You must be *exhausted* from all the effort that took."

"Yeah," joined in Duke—Tina's protector. "You're ready for the big leagues now. Maybe tomorrow you can prevent a killing spree."

Elizabeth scowled. "She's a little girl, you two. Knock it off."

"You'll see soon enough. Just wait for the teen years." Daniel took a deep breath and finally stopped laughing.

"Yeah," Duke agreed—Duke always agreed with Daniel. "There were a couple years there when Tina wouldn't listen to a damn thing I had to say. Luckily, she eventually snapped out of it."

Elizabeth cringed. It just felt so wrong when the angels swore. Besides, she didn't exactly love hearing about Tina either.

"Anyway..." Duke's voice was gravelly. Actually everything about him was gravelly, from his choice of wardrobe—ripped up jeans and a black leather vest with the Harley Davidson logo—to his raggedy salt-

and-pepper beard. "We'd better get back to the beach. We're in for a hard week just like you!"

The two resumed their raucous laughter and disappeared back into nothingness just as Nana was making her way back over to the front of the store to help Daisy pay for her rental.

It was happening again.

Daisy twirled a blond ringlet around her index finger as she flirted with the pimply-faced sales clerk at the electronics store. "So it has how much memory?" She feigned disinterest as she ran a freshly polished lavender fingernail across the box of the new iPad. The plastic snagged and crinkled.

"One-hundred and twenty-eight gigs. Doesn't get much better than this," the clerk said confidently, grabbing the box from between Daisy's hands and using it as an excuse to brush his fingers up against hers. "Should we go run this up, uhh, Miss...?"

"The name's Lizzie," Daisy said, tossing a huge—yet totally fake—smile the boy's way. "And sure, let's do it."

Elizabeth hated how Daisy used her name as an alias when she chose to do less than savory deeds, and the fact that she had once again given this assumed name could only mean…

"Stop this. You're better than this!" Elizabeth hissed with her face planted firmly into the conscience center of her daughter's brain.

Daisy batted at the air near her ears as if trying to ward away a pesky mosquito—or, as it was in this case, a butterfly—but Elizabeth persisted nonetheless.

"Don't steal it. You could ask for it on your birthday, or you could get an after school job and earn it. It will be so much better if you earn it. You'll enjoy it that much more."

Daisy stepped forward toward the register in the back of the electronics department, and her angel fell back.

"How will you be paying today, Lizzie? That's a pretty name by the way," the boy said as he scanned the barcode on the iPad's box and ran it over the demagnetizer.

"Credit. Thanks… Kyle. That's a cool name too." Daisy giggled as she let her eyes fall toward the boy's nametag. She looked him up and down while handing him her card.

Elizabeth made one last plea to her daughter's better nature. "Don't do this to yourself. You are worth more than your body. Don't steal. Don't use your sexuality as a bargaining chip."

But Daisy just continued to flirt and push her chest over the counter toward Kyle.

"Hmm," he said swiping the card a second and third time. "Machine's not taking it. Hang on one second. Let me go get my manager to approve a manual entry."

Daisy smiled innocently as Kyle stuffed the iPad in a bag, placed it under the counter, then disappeared into the back of the store.

Of course the card didn't work. It was a $5 American Express gift card she'd been carrying around for the better part of the last year. Daisy had long since spent the paltry sum on a new tube of Wet n' Wild lipstick, leaving the card devoid of any value but conveniently realistic looking enough to serve her purposes. She applied a shade of that lipstick now as a way to glance to either side in search of any remaining retail personnel.

Seeing that no one was near, she snuck behind the sales counter, grabbed the iPad from its bag, tucked it under her skirt, and walked briskly toward the exit. A minute later she was unboxing the coveted device in the driver's seat of her second-hand Camry and calling her friend on Bluetooth to brag about the masterful heist.

"Go back in the store and return it. Now. Say you took it by accident, make an excuse. It's not too late to back out!" Elizabeth warned.

Daisy backed out from her parking space without a moment's hesitation, and Elizabeth drifted back, hurt that none of her whisperings had even been acknowledged by her charge. How was she going to help Daisy reach the Gates if she insisted on doing terrible things? Sure, she was a teenager, but, back when *she* was alive, Elizabeth had never stolen a single pack of gum—let alone an expensive gadget such as the one Daisy had just taken for herself.

Daisy drove quickly toward the home she shared with Theo and Tina, and as the large box store grew more and more distant in the rearview mirror, so too did Elizabeth's vision of reuniting with her daughter on the other side of the Pearly Gates.

"Hey, we tried to warn you," Duke said when Elizabeth came to him and Daniel about the theft. "A candy bar ain't nothin' next to an iPad."

"Teenagers," Daniel added knowingly, which struck Elizabeth as odd since he had died at nine years of age.

"Will she be okay? I mean, is it too late for...?" She let her voice trail off.

"Hey, no! Don't worry, lady." Daniel insisted on calling her *lady*, no matter how many times she asked him to use her proper name. "They all go through this. It's a rite of passage or something."

"What he said. The teen years sure do make you earn those wings." Duke motioned toward Elizabeth with his chin.

Elizabeth nodded, but the moment the other two angels absconded toward their own duties she unleashed the tears that had been building within her all afternoon. What if this wasn't just a phase for Daisy? What if she died before she was able to make herself a better person, one worthy of the Gates? Elizabeth, for her part, still didn't know the exact winning formula to take her daughter from mortal to Pearl.

Whenever she asked Peter about it, he just said, "Do good. Help her to do good."

A lot of help that was, especially now that Daisy refused to listen to her, no matter how loudly or persistently the angel whispered into her conscience.

She watched as Daisy applied a large butterfly sticker to the back of her new tablet. Now it looked like everything else the girl owned, emblazoned with two large, ornate wings that stretched toward Heaven. "It's my spirit animal," she'd say whenever pressed for an answer to her butterfly obsession.

Elizabeth remained completely stumped as to why Daisy could still sometimes see her. It was not a common gift among angels, and she had no idea what triggered it. And while she was flattered her image meant so much to Daisy, she also hated that her likeness now grazed the stolen good, as if it had been ordained from above, which it most certainly had not.

A knock sounded at the door, and Tina pressed her way into the room. "What's that?" she asked as Daisy scrambled to hide the iPad under her pillow.

"Nothing."

Tina frowned and held out her hand. "Give it here, Daze."

Daisy took a deep breath, then drew the device out and handed it to her stepmother.

"Where'd you get this?"

"Tell her the truth," Elizabeth whispered. "You're a terrible liar, and besides you feel guilty about what you've done." How she wished she was in Tina's place rather than her own. There, at least, Daisy would have to acknowledge her. There, she wouldn't be invisible and mostly ignored.

Daisy twisted the corners of her frayed pillowcase between her hands, and Elizabeth could tell she was trying to buy time until she could figure out how best to proceed.

"She deserves the truth," Elizabeth said again, hating how often her job involved pushing Daisy and her replacement mother together.

"I, umm…" Daisy started.

"Yes, go on."

"I s-stole it."

Elizabeth felt an overwhelming sense of pride in her little girl. She'd done wrong, but she'd also confessed to that wrong. She'd listened to her mother, listened to her conscience. Maybe she wasn't so far gone after all.

Tina didn't say anything at first. She just held Daisy's eyes with her own. Finally, she reached over and squeezed the girl's shoulder, offered her a smile. "Thank you for telling me the truth. I know that couldn't have been easy."

Daisy frowned, a look of confusion crept across her face.

"Still," Tina continued. "What you've done *is* wrong."

"I know. I'm so sorry. I didn't mean to—"

"It's all right. I know. What I wonder though is why you didn't just ask for it. You know your birthday *is* next month, and Daddy and I would have been happy to... Anyway, what's done is done."

"Are you going to make me take it back?" Daisy's eyes shifted toward the bright polka dot rug on her floor, the one that had lain on her bedroom floor ever since she was a little girl.

"Nope." Tina plucked the iPad from Daisy's hands. "You'll get it back when you've worked it off."

"What?"

"I'll go to the store and pay for it, then you'll earn it back by completing a list of chores for me. Be warned, it's a *long* list."

Daisy's face lit from within. Her slumped frame straightened back out, and she smiled. "Thank you so much, Tina!"

The two shared a quick hug, and Elizabeth joined in the moment as well. Because, while she couldn't embrace either of them physically, she was finally ready to admit that Tina was a great mom and the perfect ally. Together they, along with Theo, would make sure their little girl turned out just right.

But she also knew her job was far from over. A life was a long time to live after all, and Elizabeth still didn't know how to unlock the combination to Heaven's Gates.

Poof!

Peter appeared beside Elizabeth, his usually somber face looking even grimmer than usual.

"You're kind of ruining the moment here," Elizabeth said, but Peter's expression remained unchanged.

"Well, what is it?"

He placed a hand on her shoulder and drew her away from Daisy's bedroom. "Come, we need to talk about the next part of the plan."

PART IV

Peter stood before Elizabeth, his stiff, sullen expression a stark contrast to the warmth of the scene that had just unfolded in Daisy's room. "It's time we discussed the next part of the plan," he said, ushering Elizabeth outside.

"Did you see that? Daisy admitted she was wrong, apologized even. It was wonderful." Elizabeth smiled wide, hoping Peter would do the same.

He did not.

"Yes, that's all very well. But—the plan. We need to discuss it, so that you're prepared for what happens next."

"What is it, Peter? I want to get back in there, and enjoy what just happened, tell Daisy what a good thing she's done, build her conscience up—basically, finish doing my job."

“Sit,” Peter instructed. “It will be better if you sit.”

Elizabeth gulped. Something was wrong, and she wasn’t quite sure she wanted to know what. She remained silent as Peter went through the next part of the plan step by step.

Peter’s voice remained deadpan despite the horrors he foretold.

“And you expect me to just accept this?” Elizabeth shouted. “To let all this happen to my daughter without fighting every step of the way?”

Peter sighed. “I’m sorry, truly sorry, but it’s not our place to question the plan. You *know* that.”

Elizabeth wanted to scream loud enough for the heavens to hear her, to demand the plan be changed, but suddenly she had no energy left to argue. Instead, she sank to the ground and wept. For how long, she couldn’t be sure, but when she pushed herself back to her feet, the sky was dark and Peter had gone.

Daniel and Duke found her later that day, their normally sunny dispositions clouded.

“He finally told you, huh?” Duke asked.

“He did, but I’m going to fight it, fight it with everything I’ve got.” Elizabeth hated that the other angels all knew of this turn before she did. She also hated that they could find her whenever they wanted, but she had no way of initiating contact with any of them. But her hatred for both these things fell short in comparison to the overwhelming rage she felt for the plan.

Well, plans could change, and in this case plans *would* change.

"What do you mean you're going to fight it? That's not how things work." Duke scratched his head and looked to Daniel.

"He's right. You see that don't you, lady? The plan is not to be messed with."

"Well, I'm messing with it. Who's going to stop me? You?"

"No one's going to stop you, because you're not going to be able to start. Don't you understand? The plan is set in stone. There's nothing you can do to break it." Daniel laid a conciliatory hand on her shoulder, and tense energy shot off him in spirals.

"So you expect me to just sit back and watch as my daughter suffers? To stand idly by as she goes through hell on earth?"

Daniel and Duke exchanged a worried look.

"Unfortunately, yeah. You can't stop her suffering, but you can comfort her as she goes through it."

"No, that's not going to be good enough. I'm going to fight this. I'm going to fight however and whomever it takes, even if it means challenging God himself."

"*Whoa*!" Duke raised his palms and backed slowly away. "She went there! She actually went there."

"Listen, lady. We like you, so we're going to pretend you didn't just go there. Yeah, it's hard. No one's saying it isn't, but what you just said... well, it's going too far, *way* too far. This conversation never happened, you hear me? *It never happened.*"

"I meant every word," Elizabeth said, biting off the end of each syllable as it left her mouth. "I *will* stop this, no matter what it takes, even if it means losing my wings."

Elizabeth kept even closer watch over Daisy than usual. It could happen at any moment, and she had to be ready. She needed to figure out how she could keep *him* away, and she needed to do it fast. If Daisy never met him, then he wouldn't be able to...

God, she couldn't even think it.

For days, Elizabeth viewed all new people with suspicion and fear—especially those of the male persuasion.

When a chatty clerk at the grocery store asked Daisy how her day was going, Elizabeth used her dodge to knock the bag of groceries out of Daisy's arms, spilling them on the floor. The clerk had to rush back to get a mop, which meant he didn't have a chance to talk to Daisy.

A few days later, a handsome barista asked for her number, and Elizabeth toppled Daisy's latte over, singeing him with hot coffee before the girl could dole out her digits.

It went on like this for weeks—months—and while Elizabeth grew weary from this hyper-vigilance, she also refused to let her guard down. She knew it would happen eventually, although she didn't know the exact time or place. And she also knew she wouldn't be able to stop the plan until it at least had the chance to get started.

The waiting was the worst part.

Pure anguish.

And Elizabeth's jumpiness had started to affect her charge as well. Now Daisy shuddered whenever anyone tried to shake her hand. She started turning down invitations to parties and spending more time at home, locked in her bedroom, scribbling away in her journal. Well, it was safer that way. Her daughter's sudden introversion was a small price to pay for keeping the plan at bay.

Daisy now clung to her journal like some teen version of a security blanket. She'd often wedge it into the spine of an open textbook and scribble away during lectures. The journal, like everything else Daisy owned, was adorned with a gold-winged butterfly.

She ran her fingertips over the embossed edges of the design as her teacher read aloud from a book of poetry by Emily Dickinson. She rarely found herself distracted during English class. It was, after all, her favorite subject. Midway through a particularly lovely poem, a sharp knock sounded on the classroom door. A moment later a tall, gangly boy loped in and cleared his throat.

"I'm, uhh, Victor Larsen. I'm new."

"Right, right. Welcome, Victor. You can take a seat in the back there next to Daisy." The teacher waited for Victor to take a seat and then carried on with his reading.

Daisy smiled as the new student sat down, and he smiled right back. After class, he asked Daisy if she wouldn't mind helping him locate his next classroom.

Warning sirens blared in Elizabeth's head.

"Daisy, no. Don't do it. He's not as nice as he seems. He will hurt you. He will ruin you," she screamed as Daisy's conscience.

Daisy shuddered, but forced a smiled. "Sure, I'd be happy to help."

"No. NO. NO!" Elizabeth screamed as loud as she could. Why wasn't the girl listening to her? This was it, the one Peter had warned her about. She was sure of it. This boy. She needed to reveal the plan if she were to have any hope of stopping it.

"Daisy, stay away from him. He's going to hurt you very badly. He will ruin your life, and eventually..." She took a deep breath. "End it. Get away while you still can, before it's too late."

Elizabeth waited for her words to take effect, only they didn't.

Daisy and Victor chatted away about music, school lunch, and the local mall. Why wasn't Daisy tripping over her feet trying to run away from him? Why wouldn't she listen?

Peter appeared and fell into step beside her as she chased the pair through the high school hallways.

"It's him, isn't it?" Elizabeth hissed, unable to tear her eyes away.

"It is."

"I knew it! I knew it! Daisy, get away from him. He's a killer!"

Daisy didn't react in the slightest.

"She can't hear you," Peter said.

"What? Why not? This sure is a hell of a time for my powers to stop working."

"Elizabeth, stop. I already told you. You can't change the plan, and you can't reveal it either. That's why she didn't hear you when you tried to tell her about it."

She paused and looked to Peter whose face was arranged into a scowl. "But… I know we have the power to stop this from happening. We must. We just have to figure out how, and—"

"There's nothing we can do. I'm sorry."

"No, you're not!" Elizabeth spat. "You're not sorry at all. If you were, you'd help me find a way to keep her safe. You probably have no idea what it's like, do you? Being forced to watch as the person you love most in this world walks into a terrible trap? You never loved anyone. You just don't—"

Peter cut her off with a string of shaky words she could barely make out. "That's… not… true."

"What? What did you say?"

Peter had stopped walking, so she fell back with him, still keeping her eyes on Daisy and the monster beside her.

"I know exactly what it's like. Even better than you do as a matter of fact, because it's already happened to me. I watched as she died a sudden, painful death. I wanted to save her, but I couldn't. It's not our place. So *please* would you stop accusing me of not caring?"

Peter rubbed at the beginnings of tears, which made Elizabeth very uncomfortable. He was supposed to be the strong one, the one who presented facts instead of feelings. Had he once been just like her?

She risked another quick glance away from Daisy to fix her eyes on him. "Peter, were you once a protector?"

He held his hands up as if to indicate the matter was not up for discussion. "Please," he repeated and that single word provided more insight into his humanity than anything he'd said before.

"Okay. But if you truly understand, can you help me see it too? Why does this have to happen? Daisy hasn't done anything wrong, certainly not wrong enough to deserve this. Why should she have to suffer when there are terrible people out there living without a worry in the world?"

"You want to know why bad things happen to good people."

Elizabeth nodded. "And why good things happen to bad people. Why can't it be more fair?"

"In time, everyone gets their due. Don't worry about those who do evil. They will be dealt with, just not by you." Peter shifted to focus his gaze on Daisy, and they watched her together for a few moments. Elizabeth had assumed he'd forgotten to answer the other part of her question when suddenly he spoke again.

"Bad things—especially when they happen to good people—accelerate the soul's journey. They mean less waiting to get to the Gates. And those 'bad things' are a blessing, whether or not they seem that way at first. I know it's hard to understand, especially when someone you love is hurting, but it's the truth."

Elizabeth didn't know what to say, so she remained silent.

"Your job will be to ease her suffering, and I know you'll do well. Godspeed, Elizabeth," Peter vanished.

She'd gone out on dates with Victor a few times now, and nothing bad had happened. So far. Elizabeth knew deep within her heart that Victor was the one she had been warned about—warned and then told she could do nothing to stop him. As it turned out, the afterlife was every bit as unfair as mortal life had been. Even more so, perhaps.

Daisy spritzed vanilla body spray on the inside of each wrist and then rubbed it behind her ears, a trick Tina had taught her. She placed butterfly studs into each ear lobe, and then eased on a pair of stiletto heels her father still had no idea she owned. As she worked to create a smoky eye, Elizabeth used her dodge to knock a picture from the dresser. It fell and shattered on the hardwood floor below.

"Shoot!" Daisy mumbled under her breath as she bent to sweep the glass fragments into her hands.

Elizabeth realized only after it fell that the picture was of her and Theo on their wedding day. How much had changed since that day nearly twenty years ago. Maybe it was poetic, the picture falling to its doom only moments before Elizabeth would fail as a protector, the fate of her charge splintering into a million broken pieces.

You can only ease her suffering, both Daniel and Peter had said. *It's your job to make the fallout easier.*

Daisy was fighting back tears as she stroked the aged portrait of her mother's face. Elizabeth wanted to cry too. Everything was ruined, or it soon would be. She made one final half-hearted attempt to fling Daisy's hand from the doorknob as she pulled it open and strolled outside to meet Victor.

He took her to the movies, some action flick. Elizabeth didn't pay much attention, and neither did they instead choosing to make out in the darkened theater as if they could suck life-giving oxygen from each other's lungs.

They reluctantly pulled apart when the film ended and the lights snapped back on. The credits were now over too, and everyone else had already cleared out of the theater.

"Come home with me," Victor said, a demand not a request.

Daisy giggled. "I don't think your parents will like that very much."

He bit her earlobe then whispered the next part into her hair. "They're out for the night, some charity ball. We'll have the place all to ourselves."

"NO!" Elizabeth yelled, also leaning into Daisy's hair so she could speak directly into her conscience.

She hated how close she was to Victor in that moment, but it was a necessary evil.

Daisy bit her lip and then mumbled, "Okay."

Elizabeth shouted into her head the entire drive from the theater to Victor's sprawling suburban mansion. Even though Peter had explained that all attempts to reveal the plan before its time would fall on deaf ears, Elizabeth tried anyway.

"This is bad, Daisy. Really, really bad. He will hurt you. This one decision will ruin your entire life. Run away from him. Run far, far away."

But Daisy didn't hear—or at least she didn't listen. Instead she accepted a tumbler full of red wine Victor had filched from his parents' collection.

"Why so tense? It's only me." He flashed a serpentine smile and then pulled her onto his lap while he worked at massaging the knots from Daisy's shoulders.

"Mmm. That feels so good," Daisy moaned.

"You think that feels good?" Victor laughed and flipped her around on his lap. "Try this."

And they were kissing even hotter and heavier than before.

He slipped his hand up her shirt, and she pulled away as if she'd been burned.

"Hey, hey," he whispered sweet like poison. "It's okay."

Daisy nodded and allowed him to pull her shirt over her head. A few moments later he unhooked her bra and threw it onto the floor.

Elizabeth wanted to puke, but instead she wept. Her voice had abandoned her, which meant she could only watch in fear as she waited for it to happen. She clamped her eyes shut but stayed close by in case Daisy needed her.

Now Victor pushed down the waistband of her pants.

She drew in a deep breath but didn't protest as he helped her out of her pants and underwear and then guided her hands to his belt.

Elizabeth knew everything that was happening despite her best efforts to tune it out. And she knew the exact moment when new life bloomed within her daughter's womb, an innocent new life hitching itself to Daisy's, and Daisy's lifeline tying itself forever to her captor's, to a boy whose potential for evil was far from met.

PART V

Daisy's baby didn't have its own angel yet, which meant Elizabeth was hopelessly alone. When she'd asked where Victor's protector was, Peter murmured something about wardens before snapping his fingers and fading back into the ether.

It had all happened so fast: Daisy missing her period and deciding to take an at-home pregnancy test; learning of the baby and confiding her secret to Tina; the two of them then telling Theo together; Victor showing up at the house unannounced and asking for Daisy's hand in marriage, along with the chance to prove himself. These events, while separate, hung together in Elizabeth's memory in one giant swirl of time that had passed far too quickly.

One moment that stood out clear and sharp against the rest was the courthouse where they had all stood together in the judge's chambers. The simple ceremony couldn't have lasted more than two minutes. Victor said, *I do.* Daisy said, *I do.* They exchanged cheap gold bands, and—just like that—Daisy shed her father's name and assumed that of her captor.

Why did this particular end have so many beginnings? Elizabeth wondered. She watched in silence as her daughter hugged first Tina and then Mrs. Larsen. The unfamiliar woman remained stiff throughout the proceedings and didn't even raise her arms to reciprocate Daisy's hug. As if it were Daisy's fault the woman's son was such a careless Casanova; as if it were his life that had been ruined by Daisy and not the other way around.

But Elizabeth knew better. She'd seen the plan, and even though she knew she couldn't stop it, she still tried, like a movie-goer shouting at the screen to warn the hero not to enter the darkened room. Daisy had already placed both feet firmly into the dark and eerie future. The killer lay in wait, ready to end his unassuming victim.

But nobody else knew the future, not yet anyway. They all continued to hug—except stodgy Mrs. Larsen—and exchange well-wishes.

If only, if only…

Elizabeth could no longer watch, so she focused her vision on Theo, the husband she had lost. It wasn't just Daisy who'd be leaving home, after all; Elizabeth, too, had to say goodbye to all she'd ever known.

They moved in together later that same day. Victor's parents had purchased a tiny trailer on the edge of town, which Elizabeth feared was their way of maintaining control without having to actually move the young couple and their future infant into their own home.

And the very next day, as if to prove her suspicions correct, Mrs. Larsen stopped by unannounced, a ficus plant clutched between her finely manicured fingers. "I thought the place could use a little extra life," she announced in a false vibrato.

"Thanks," Daisy mumbled. "Victor's just at—"

"At school, I know. Finishing his education up the way God intended it."

Oh, how Elizabeth wished she could intervene, could wrap Daisy in her arms and cover her ears while she yelled obscenities at this horrible woman. It wasn't Daisy's fault her lascivious son couldn't keep his pants on. At least, the two children shared in the blame. At worst, Victor was the tempter in this situation; Daisy the lovesick girl only trying to keep him happy by giving him what he wanted. Besides, she didn't need school where she was going.

Elizabeth shuddered at how casually that thought popped up. No, she was not accepting the plan. Not yet. Not ever.

Mrs. Larsen stopped in often, soon dropping the façade of bringing some gift item the trailer positively required to be habitable. Daisy seemed annoyed by her new mother-in-law's constant comings and goings, but always treated the older woman with a kindness that, frankly, she didn't deserve.

Was Elizabeth the only one who noticed that Mrs. Larsen never brought any gifts for the baby? In fact, she never even mentioned the baby at all. Most of her talk was mundane—how things were so wonderful and magnificent in her world, what a good boy Victor was, and, of course, how much more Daisy needed to be doing to keep up her end of … whatever this was.

One day, Daisy invited Tina over to help break up the monotony that was quickly becoming her life, and

Tina arrived with a brown paper bag topped to the brim with yarn, ribbon, and other crafting implements.

"I've been working on an afghan for the baby, but then I realized I could teach you to knit too. It's such a relaxing hobby—and practical too. Want me to show you how to make some booties?" Tina asked while unpacking the contents of the bag onto the coffee table.

Daisy nodded vigorously and gave her a tight hug. "I've missed you and Daddy so much."

A look of concern crossed Tina's face. "Married life not quite what you expected?"

"Actually—"

But Daisy's confession was cut short by the arrival of—who else?—Mrs. Larsen. Daisy dropped the skein of yarn in her lap and stood clumsily to her feet. The bulge in her belly had started to become noticeable these last few weeks.

"Hi, Mrs. Larsen. You remember my mom Tina, right?"

"Yes." She sat opposite them in the armchair and crossed her legs at the knee.

Tina spoke next, "I was just starting up a knitting lesson with Daisy. I have an extra pair of needles if you'd like to learn too."

"No, thank you," came the curt reply. She scooped her phone out of her handbag and set to typing furiously onto its tiny screen. All attempts at conversation from either Tina or Daisy went largely ignored. Yet the woman refused to budge, refused to give them any privacy.

When at last Tina left, Mrs. Larsen popped up and began to riffle through the contents of the fridge. "Victor will be hungry when he comes home. Let's get a nice stew going."

Daisy shrugged but followed her into the kitchen and filled a pot with water for the potatoes.

Mrs. Larsen set to work on the onions, pausing occasionally to wipe away a stray tear. "Do me a favor, dear?"

Daisy perked up. "Need a dish for those onions?"

"No, it's not that." She wiped her hands off on a paper towel. "I don't want that woman stopping by anymore." She said it so casually as if she'd asked for the girl to pass salt across the table.

Elizabeth was flabbergasted.

Daisy didn't seem to know how to respond either. "What? Tina? But she's my mom."

"Don't say things that aren't true." Mrs. Larsen

scowled, then quickly switched to a pleasant smile. "Your mother's dead, dear."

The two women continued to cook together in silence. Elizabeth tried to use her dodge to get Daisy to smack the woman across her gaunt cheek, but Daisy refused to cooperate.

"This isn't right, and you know it," the angel whispered into Daisy's conscience. "You need to tell Victor what his mother said, how she's been treating you. You are nobody's doormat." But even as Elizabeth said it, she worried Daisy's pleas would fall on deaf ears.

Sure enough, as the two were getting ready for bed—long after they'd finished their supper and Mrs. Larsen had excused herself—Daisy explained the weird request his mother had made. But rather than take offense on her behalf, Victor just sighed.

"I'd do what she says. The Larsens are from better stock, and she just wants what's best for her grandchild. You can understand that, can't you?"

Daisy frowned and turned away from Victor in bed, and he did nothing to comfort her. Funny, Elizabeth thought, that Victor had no idea how little his mother cared for anyone but herself. Would she continue to ignore the baby's very existence once it was free of its mother's womb? A living, breathing, physical thing?

Ever since the Tina incident, Mrs. Larsen had taken to escorting Daisy on the few occasions she needed to leave the trailer. Victor, of course, carried on as if nothing in his life had changed. He still went to school, to sports practice, hung out with friends, came home and logged a few hours on his X-Box before calling it a night.

He was happy as could be—any complaints from Daisy but a blip on the radar of his otherwise smooth and peaceful life.

Daisy on the other hand was suffering, mostly in silence. In the still of the night, she contemplated throwing herself down a flight of stairs or sticking a hanger up into her insides. It wasn't that she wanted to kill the baby, but what would life be like for it, living under the constant judgment of the Larsens? Daisy was still young, full of potential, save this one thing.

But she didn't have it in her to harm a fly, let alone her own child. So instead she blamed herself—for having unprotected sex, for agreeing to marry

Victor, for not trying harder to stand up to Mrs. Larsen, for all of it.

In fact, the baby was the one thing that brought her comfort. Well, as far as she knew. Elizabeth was always there, whispering soothing affirmations into her soul.

You are a good person.

Things will get better.

It's okay.

For what else could the angel say? She wasn't allowed to speak of the plan, and she couldn't bring herself to lie. So she stuck to whispering these platitudes, day and night, as often as her charge needed to hear them to keep from breaking down in tears.

But today things would be better. Today she was going to find out the sex of the baby, or so she thought. She giggled as the ultrasound tech slathered the cool gel on her belly and slid the sensor back and forth. At twenty weeks, the baby now had a discernable human form—a button nose, fingers, that persistent, beating heart.

"Do you want to know whether you're having a boy or a girl?" The tech asked with a smile.

"That won't be necessary," Mrs. Larsen intruded. "We prefer to be surprised, the way God intended."

The tech shrugged and tossed a look of sympathy Daisy's way.

Daisy closed her eyes to keep the tears from escaping.

Finally Daisy decided to fight for herself. When Victor came home that evening, she stood in front of the TV, refusing to budge until they talk.

"Your mom really upset me today," she started, recounting the whole scene at the obstetrician's office.

Victor listened in silence, his posture suggesting that her concerns were but a minor annoyance in his otherwise perfect day.

"And besides," Daisy continued, gathering confidence. "What's with her *always* being around? I married you, not your mom, but it seems like I spend way more time with her. You're never here, and when you are, your attention is somewhere else. Don't you love me?"

"Of course, I love you. Why would you even ask that question?" Victor stood, still seeming far away.

"Because I'm not happy," Daisy sobbed.

Victor finally came forward and wrapped his young wife in a hug.

She smiled, feeling braver than when the conversation had begun. "If you could just talk to your mother, ask her to back off a bit. I think—"

Victor ripped away, his eyes darted back and forth as he studied her as if he could not recognize who she'd become. "Back off? Back off? Like my mother is some kind of imposition to you?"

Daisy knotted her fingers together and stared at a pasta sauce stain on the floor.

"I can't believe this," Victor exploded. "She's just doing all this because she cares about you. You're lucky she welcomed you into the family with such open arms. You think she liked the idea of me throwing my life away to marry you? No, but she's making the best of it."

"I'm just trying to tell you how I feel," Daisy said in barely more than a whisper.

"Well, the way you feel is *wrong*. Damn it, Daisy. What the hell?"

Daisy's bottom lip trembled. She tried so hard not to cry, to remain strong and demand the respect that she—that all people—deserved.

But Victor was just getting warmed up. "God, how did I ever fall for such a stupid girl in the first place? Doesn't know how good she has it. Instead just bitches and moans at every opportunity. Are you finished? Because I don't have time for this bullshit." He moved toward her, ready to push her out of the way so he could turn on the TV, get back to his game.

But Elizabeth saw it coming and managed a dodge just in time. He didn't lay a hand on Daisy, but still her heart had been badly hurt.

She continued down the hall and let herself into the bathroom, where she eventually fell asleep huddled on the floor, tears streaming down her face.

Daisy crept out from the bathroom when she was sure Victor had nodded off for the night. She fished her phone from the counter and let herself outside to make the call.

Theo picked up after the third ring, sleep apparent in his voice. "Daisy? What's wrong?"

"Daddy," she whispered so that Victor wouldn't hear. "Please could you come get me?"

"I'll be right there."

She ran into his arms the moment he arrived.

"Daisy," he mumbled into her hair. "Please, please tell me what's wrong."

"I'm not ready."

"Not ready for what?"

"To be a wife, a mom. I'm not ready for any of this. Please take me back."

Elizabeth wished they could all go back in time several months, back before any of this had happened, before the plan had begun to unfold. But for now, all Theo could do is return their daughter to her childhood home—which he did gladly.

The next morning, Theo prepared Mickey Mouse pancakes with chocolate chips, and the three of them sat at the table, munching away as if nothing had changed. When in fact, everything had changed.

As Theo was frying up a second batch on the griddle, a soft knock sounded on the door. Moments later, Mrs. Larsen appeared in the kitchen and motioned for Daisy to come with her.

Tina wrapped her stepdaughter in a hug. "You know you have a home with us as long as you need one, right?" she whispered under the watchful eye of Mrs. Larsen.

Daisy nodded. "It's fine. Victor and I had a little fight, but I know he loves me."

"Yes," Mrs. Larsen added. "And he's very worried about you. We best be going."

Daisy kissed both Tina and her father before leaving.

"Victor was worried sick about you," Mrs. Larsen said as they both buckled themselves into her luxury SUV. She drove in silence—no further reprimands, no small talk, no radio—as if to give Daisy time to think about what she had done.

Elizabeth hoped Daisy knew that she had done the right thing, that she could—and should—leave again, that the trailer was no home to her, the Larsens no family.

They pulled up in front of the trailer, and Daisy got out.

Mrs. Larsen drove away without so much as a good-bye.

Victor pounced on his wife as soon as she entered the doorway. "It's funny," he said in a tone that suggested no humor in what he was about to say. "That you'd be the one to try to leave when you're the one who's so lucky. I didn't have to stay. I didn't have to marry you, you stupid bitch. If it weren't for me, you'd be on the streets, selling your body to feed yourself and your bastard kid. You know that?"

Daisy's eyes were wide like an owl's, her mouth held firmly shut.

"But, no, I married you, even though I didn't have to, and I'm here to be a father to your kid, even though I don't have to. And what do you do?" His voice boomed even louder. He paced back and forth, running his hands through his hair.

"You run off like I'm some loser. Like you're the one who got the short end of the stick in this—" He gestures around their homey trailer. "This arrangement … You embarrassed me really bad, Daisy. How could you go and do that?"

When Daisy didn't answer, Victor let out a raspy, angry sigh. "Unbelievable," he muttered. "Can't even say sorry. Aargh!" He made a fist, and Daisy flinched, squeezing her eyes shut, bracing for impact.

When she opened them again, she saw the hole in the drywall behind them, Victor nursing his reddened knuckles, refusing to look at her.

"Now look what you made me do."

"I- I- I'm sorry," Daisy stammered. "I'm so sorry."

Daisy lay awake that night, waiting for Victor to come to bed, to have his way with her, fall into a series of soft snores beside her—the whole time wondering when, *when* would things get better.

"It won't be long now, baby girl," Elizabeth whispered, for once thankful for the plan, that her daughter's suffering would soon be put to an end. It only had to get a little bit worse first, then everything could be better.

When she was certain Victor had entered a deep sleep, Daisy tiptoed out into the night wearing only her oversized pajama shirt. She'd resolved to tell her parents everything, to ask them for help in getting away from the Larsens once and for all.

Things would be better, she'd decided. And she was right, but not in the way she assumed.

As her hand wrapped around the knob to the door that stood between her captivity and freedom, the lamp shot on like lightning in the night sky.

Seconds later, Victor's arms wrapped around her from behind.

She kicked at him, scratched him, did her best to get away, but he was so much stronger and she was uncoordinated because of the pregnancy. She twisted and turned, but he only held tighter, meeting each of her blows with one that was doubly forceful.

Then came the blood, so much blood. Victor let go, fell back, mumbled, "Daze, I'm sorry. I don't know what… Oh, God! Daze, are you okay? It was an accident… I didn't mean to… I mean, I don't know how…"

Daisy pushed past him and fled to the bathroom.

Victor fell to the ground, his head in his hands as he cried—more afraid for himself than his injured wife and child, Elizabeth suspected.

It's okay, my baby. It's okay, she whispered.

But Daisy was terrified. She mopped up the blood with a towel and sat down in the bathtub, rocking back and forth, growing weaker by the second.

And Elizabeth stayed by her side the whole time, because she couldn't change the plan, could only bring comfort as it unfolded.

Hush now. Everything will be all right.

At some point Victor left for school, gently rasping on the door to tell Daisy goodbye, that he was sorry, that he loved her.

Elizabeth couldn't be sure that Daisy had heard though. She was so weak.

By the time Victor returned that evening, his wife lay dead in a puddle of her own blood. She never even got to find out that her baby had been a girl.

Everything faded to white.

"Is it over?" Elizabeth asked Peter who now stood before her in the familiar place amidst the clouds. "Have I failed?"

Peter gave her a hug, a gesture he'd never made to her before. "It's far from over. Come, there's somebody I'd like you to meet."

PART VI

Peter beckoned for Elizabeth to come with him. She glanced back at her daughter's corpse in the tub surrounded by a pink pool of bath water mixed with blood. Her head slumped against her shoulder; her eyes were closed but her mouth was parted slightly. It almost seemed as if Daisy were sleeping, as if she would wake up at any moment, healthy and happy again. Perhaps they could wake up a year ago, back before any of these terrible events had begun to unfold.

"Come with me," Peter urged, and Elizabeth turned away from Daisy, realizing she would never see her again—nor would she ever see the granddaughter who had died inside of her. Both their lives had ended before they'd really ever had the chance to begin.

Elizabeth had failed as a protector.

Peter returned them to the nebulous in-between. "There's someone I'd like you to meet," he said. Everything was white, but Elizabeth could still see the imprint of the gory scene they'd just left. Somehow she felt it would always be there waiting for her, just on the insides of her eyelids.

Once again time disappeared as they floated through the clouds. Whether she'd been separated from Daisy for an eternity or but a fleeting moment, Elizabeth couldn't say. Somehow both felt true.

"Are you ready?" Peter asked. He snapped his fingers and the vast whiteness around them transformed. Walls around them formed a tiny ranch-style house. From the looks of the décor, they were now somewhere in the American Southwest.

A baby cried, and Elizabeth knew.

She rushed to the bedroom down the hall, Peter following close behind.

"Elizabeth, this is—"

"I know," she responded before he could finish. "It's her." Happiness swelled in her heart as she studied the naked infant rooting about for her mother's nipple. And suddenly Elizabeth felt whole again. She hadn't realized how badly the absence hurt until that special place in her heart was filled once again. An angel without a charge no longer, her purpose had returned.

"This is Floramaria," Peter explained softly. "It seems you've already recognized her spirit. When her last body died, her soul came here for another chance at the Gates."

Elizabeth had tears in her eyes. "I'd know her anywhere." The baby's dark hair and tiny form looked so unlike the Daisy she'd left behind, but there was no mistaking the energy that surrounded her, the gleam behind her tiny nearsighted eyes.

"You see," Peter continued. "The spirit cannot be broken. It cannot be killed. It will always fight to survive in one form or another until the day it can return to its Maker."

"To Heaven, you mean? Through the Gates?"

"That's precisely what I mean."

"It was so hard to watch her die. I wish I'd known…" Elizabeth sucked in a deep breath. While it was true she no longer *needed* to take in oxygen, mimicking such human gestures often brought a special kind of calm—one she needed now.

Peter sighed, too. "It never gets any easier. Each death will be impossibly heartbreaking, but each new birth impossibly joyful."

"So how many does it take? How many lives until we can be together again?"

"It's different for every person. When Daisy—when Floramaria—has learned all humanity has to offer, that's when her soul will be complete. That's when she can return, and you with her."

"And that's it? She'll die and be reborn until she's good enough for Heaven?"

"More or less." Peter's voice dropped to a whisper. "With a few exceptions."

"Exceptions?"

"Never you mind that. Look, she's opening her eyes. Go to her. She'll be able to see you again. Remember? She's still close to the other realm. She can sense things adults cannot. Comfort her now. She needs you just as she always will."

And with that Peter vanished.

Elizabeth's new home was filled with joy in the months that followed Floramaria's birth, a pleasant difference from how the time following Daisy's birth—and her own death—had been. She enjoyed being part of this new family. Floramaria was the third child but first girl, and everyone doted on her—not just the immediate family, but the extended one as well.

A constant stream of visitors flowed through the cramped living room, bringing home-cooked meals and telling stories, watching Floramaria as she learned to crawl. Her brothers, as they played nearby, kept watch over the newest member of the family. Elizabeth was happy her daughter had found such a good home the second time around, but also saddened by the fact that she hadn't been the one to provide it for her.

She thought often of Theo and Tina, of how their lives must be in the wake of Daisy's death, of what things would have been like for them all without the arrival of the Larsens, what things could have been like had she never died in the first place, had she been allowed to raise her daughter the way nature intended.

A few months after Floramaria and Elizabeth joined the family, the other angels decided to announce themselves—and they formed a veritable choir, the four of them plus Elizabeth together.

"I'm Julio," one of them said. "She's mine." He pointed to the wife. "Alexis here looks after him, and Naomi and Vlad watch the boys. Not a lot tends to happen. And, hey, that's for the best, right? So, anyway, tell us about you. Tell us about the new girl.

You are a *protector*, aren't you? You look like a protector. Not one of those…"

"Julio, hush," Alexis warned as if they too were some sort of married couple.

"One of those what?" Elizabeth asked. She hated being the last to know, especially given what had happened the last time other angels had attempted to keep a secret from her—that had been the beginning of the end for Daisy. As far as she knew now, there was no plan. Although *obviously* there was a plan, it just wasn't known to any of the angels yet. She hoped this time Peter would confide in her first. Was that too much to ask?

"It's nothing." Alexis shot Julio a dirty look. "He just meant the wardens, and you're clearly not one of them."

The other four angels shuddered.

"What are the—?"

"See?" Alexis gloated. "She doesn't even know what they are. You must be a baby angel, huh? How many births has little Floramaria had before this one?"

"Just one."

"Oh, wow! You *are* young. You probably even remember your human life, don't you?"

"Yes, I—"

Alexis eyed her with contempt. "Well, be careful about that! Angels like you can really do a number on their charges."

"Hey, that's not fair!" Elizabeth felt meek and foolish, something neither Daniel nor Duke had ever done to her. She missed them now, almost as much as she missed her human family.

"This is true," Vlad said with a thick Slavic accent. "You hear stories of what they call *past life regression*? Is no regression, ha! Is angel refusing to let go."

"They make a point," Naomi said, with a look of sympathy. "It may seem great to be able to go back, but, believe me, it's not. Do Floramaria a favor and let it all go. It'll be doing a favor for yourself, too."

"Well, I think we've done enough damage here," Alexis said. "We should really be going."

All the other angels snapped to attention, ready to follow Alexis's lead.

"We'll see you soon, okay?" Julio said, patting her on the shoulder before they all disappeared.

Elizabeth tried to put the strange encounter with the other angels behind her, but the more she puzzled over their cryptic warnings, the more she found herself missing the life she had left behind.

She enjoyed dancing for Floramaria and making silly faces as she hovered near the baby's bouncer. Above all else, she loved hearing the little girl's laugh. Laughter, she realized, belonged to the soul—because it sounded exactly the same coming from Floramaria as it once had from Daisy.

And she laughed often. The big, loving family made sure of it.

But the more she sat by and watched the happy married couple snuggle up on the sofa for date night or sit down together at the table for a home-cooked meal, the more she found herself longing for Theo.

The other angels didn't visit her often, and whenever they did, they mostly stuck to bickering with each other and wondering aloud about Elizabeth's past rather than providing any actual companionship. This meant she missed not only Theo, but also his angel Daniel. Daniel had always done right by her, had been a friend to her when no one else would.

Peter came to visit her every so often, but their talks focused largely on her duties and Floramaria's progression through life and toward the Gates. Any time she tried to talk about her feelings, Peter would provide a terse reply and either redirect the conversation or disappear altogether.

Watching the family's happiness had become a double-edged sword. Their bliss cast a light on all that was missing from her existence.

Daniel. Duke. Tina. Theo. Who she once had been.

But the speculation, the loneliness, the vicarious joy—it had all fashioned itself into her new normal. She thought nothing of it until Floramaria began to mumble her first words.

"Mama," she said, and her parents oohed and ahhed and sent mass texts to the family to share this important milestone.

"Papa," she said, and they were every bit as proud.

"Tio," the baby said. "Tio, Tio, *Tio*." Every time she would fix her eyes on Elizabeth and smile as the syllables escaped her tiny mouth.

"You want Tio Rodrigo, Flora?" her mother asked, then excitedly called her favorite brother over to see his niece who was asking for him by name.

"*Digametio*? Can you say *Uncle Rodrigo*?" The parents prompted.

"Tio," Floramaria said proudly, pounding on the coffee table and smiling Elizabeth's way.

"Yes, that's right, baby! *Me llamo Tio* Rodrigo."

The baby shook her head and pointed to the corner of the room where Elizabeth sat watching the exchange. "Tio!" she said emphatically.

And that's when Elizabeth knew for certain. Floramaria wasn't asking for her uncle, but rather for *Theo.*

What would happen when the little girl learned to enunciate her *th*? Would the family take any of this seriously?

She thought back on the other angels' warnings and felt frightened, until she realized what this new turn of events could mean. It meant Floramaria could build a bridge between their former lives and this new one. She could bring them back to Theo, help tell him that both of his girls were okay, that they'd both moved on to new existences, that they'd see him again someday beyond the Gates.

The question remained, though. Would Floramaria's new parents help the little girl find her former father, and would he believe that she knew him? *They would*, because Elizabeth would do whatever it took to make sure this opportunity didn't pass any of them by.

PART VII

What had started as a tiny spark of anxiety quickly ignited into a raging fire—a thing of both beauty and danger. Floramaria had simply asked for Theo initially, but quickly moved on to more specific discussions of her past life. The little girl placed her hand on her tummy. "I hope my baby will be a girl," she said, tenderly rubbing her flat abdomen. "It would be nice to have a daughter. I hope Victor thinks so, too."

"*Mija*, who's this Victor?" the father asked. He turned to his wife and whispered, "Do we know a Victor?" Like Elizabeth, her earthly parents had become quite worried—even more so, given they did not understand the reasons behind their daughter's strange behavior.

"We need to see Daddy. He will explain everything."

"I'm right here, Floramaria, but I have no idea what you're talking about."

The little girl blew a raspberry and rolled her eyes. "Not you, Daddy. *Theo.* I used to be Daisy, but then I died. There was a lot of blood. When I woke up again, I was Flora, but inside I'm still Daisy, too."

Husband and wife exchanged a nervous look and put on their daughter's favorite TV show to distract everyone from the frightening things she was saying.

At night, after tucking all their children into bed, they spoke again.

"It's getting worse by the day. What should we do?"

"I think we have to find this Theo person for the answer. It seems the only way."

Floramaria's mother crossed herself and muttered a prayer. "I'm scared for her. I'm scared for us. Do you think it's a curse from a demon?"

He took her in his arms. "No, baby, no. She's just a little girl."

"That's what scares me so much."

They held each other for a long time but said no more.

In the morning, they dropped their sons off at Tio's and strapped Floramaria firmly into her booster seat.

"Are we going to find my first daddy?" the girl asked, a huge grin on her face.

The palpable tension that filled the car told Elizabeth the answer long before either parent said a word.

Her mother spoke first. "If we go and see Theo, will you drop all this nonsense?"

"It's not nonsense. It's just what… what I remember."

"Answer your mother's question, *Mija*."

Flora nodded vigorously. "Yes, yes, I promise."

They pulled away from the curb. "Do you know how to find him?"

Daisy nodded again. "His name is Theo Smith, and he lives at 2080 Mulberry Lane."

"In Texas?" Her mother asked, finally joining in the conversation. Elizabeth noticed how she twisted and wrung an embroidered hanky in her hands while she stared blankly ahead.

Flora shook her head as she positioned her favorite blonde-haired dolly onto the seat beside her. "Michigan."

"But, *Mija*, that is so far! Maybe we can call him instead."

"No!" Floramaria looked up from beneath a furled brow. "I need to see him to make sure he understands."

"Understands what, Flora?"

She shook her head from side to side. "I need to tell *him*. Sorry, Mama. Sorry, Papa." She jutted out her lower lip, then whispered, "You still love me right?"

"Of course, we love you, Mija. And, of course, we will go to see this Theo if that's what you think you need to do." The corners of his eyes crinkled in a smile as his vision shifted to his daughter in the rearview mirror.

His wife did not smile. Quite the opposite. "But we can't just—"

"Hush, it is decided. We'll take a long weekend. It will be nice to have a little road trip, just the three of us."

Floramaria and her father carried on a string of broken conversation as they drove, while the mother remained quiet, seething with anger, fear, or perhaps both.

Elizabeth watched and waited. She tried to think of what the reunion would be like, but she really had no idea what to expect. Would Theo believe the little girl's claims to be the daughter he'd lost? Would Flora repeat what Elizabeth had whispered into her conscience and deliver her own messages to Theo? It was impossible to say.

As the terrain changed from desert sands to winter snow, Floramaria began to bounce in her seat. Her broad smile clearly unnerved her parents, but she was too excited—and far too innocent—to notice. She was coming home, Elizabeth realized. For she too felt more and more at ease as the journey continued. No matter what the other angels said, this was right—it had to be.

Flora would just tell her that they were both okay, then he could move on, they could move on. Everyone would be so much happier.

To Elizabeth, it seemed no time at all before they arrived. Funny how being an angel removed all sense of time. Whether she'd died a moment ago or a thousand years back, the only point of reference Elizabeth maintained was the young soul who now went by Floramaria but who'd once been her daughter, Daisy.

They arrived in front the house Elizabeth knew so well. The white shutters had since been painted over with a handsome forest green but little else had changed.

"What will we say to these people?" the mother asked with her hand frozen over her seatbelt buckle.

"Don't worry, Mama. I know just what to say." Floramaria skipped from the vehicle before either of her parents had exited and let herself right into the home that had once been hers.

Elizabeth attempted to use her dodge to stop Flora, but the little girl moved too quickly even for her extracorporeal form.

"Ease into it," she whispered into her charge's heart. "Don't scare them."

"I won't," the girl answered back, shocking Elizabeth and drawing slack-jawed stares from her parents who stood in the open doorway.

Elizabeth was startled by the girl's words. It was almost as if, she… Impossible. She didn't have time to analyze what had happened, not when the big moment she had waited for so patiently was now unfolding before her.

"Anton…" Tina's familiar voice rang out from the living room. "Close the door. You'll let the flies in!"

"But, Mama, I'm right here," a little boy, who appeared to be roughly seven years of age, called from the floor. He kept his head down as he pushed racecars along a track.

"Then who…?" Tina dropped her eReader to her lap and craned her neck toward the open door.

"It's me, Daisy. I came home," the little girl said, stepping forward.

Tina's dark skin lost some of its luster as she moved to stand in front of the boy. "Daisy's d-dead."

Flora giggled. "No, I'm not. I'm right here."

"Mama?" the boy tugged on the hem of Tina's dress. "Who's Daisy? Have I met her before?"

Tina opened her mouth to answer, but the words seemed stuck.

"Flora, get back here." Her mother spoke firmly.

The father took a step forward. "Mrs. Smith? Pardon us. This is our daughter Floramaria. She believes she knows you. It's all very strange, but we mean no harm. May we come in?"

"How do you know my name? How do you know Daisy?"

"It's a long story, and we're not even sure we understand it all ourselves. Please can we come in? We've driven very far to meet with you."

"Theo?" Tina called. Her voice wavered, but her body stood stock straight. "Could you please come down here? We have company."

Nobody spoke until Theo emerged from his office and descended the stairs, a huge, welcoming smile on his face. "Hello, I'm Theo. How can I help you?"

Floramaria ran up to him and wrapped her arms around his legs in a huge hug. "Daddy, don't you recognize me?" Tears formed at the corner of her nut-brown eyes.

"Recognize you? I'm sorry, but we haven't met before."

Flora sniffed. "Yes, we have. It's been a while since everything happened with Victor and the baby, but it's still me. You haven't forgotten me, have you?"

Theo stiffened and moved himself away from the child. "What kind of sick joke is this?"

"It's not a joke, sir. She's been speaking of you for years, says you were her daddy before."

"My daughter is dead."

"No, Daddy, I didn't die, and neither did Mom. She is right here with me. She's an angel now."

Theo's face grew red. "First you demean the memory of my daughter, and then my wife? Who are you, and why are you doing this?" His voice shook.

"We're very sorry, sir. We didn't mean to cause you any pain. Your family is all she can talk about. We thought maybe it was God's will we should meet, but we can see now it was wrong. Again we are so very sorry. Flora, come. Let's go home." Her father motioned for her to exit through the still-open door, but the girl dug her feet into the carpet and crossed her arms over her chest.

"I'm not lying!" she shouted. "Why won't anyone believe me?"

"I believe you," Anton said, rising. "I had a different Daddy before too, but he died and so did my first Mommy. Do you want to play cars with me?"

"Anton, n-no. D-d-don't." Tina could barely speak for all the tears that were choking her voice.

Elizabeth hoped Theo would think about all the girl had said and know that she and their daughter were doing just fine. Still, she was now less certain than ever if what she had done was right. Had it only caused more pain? Reopened old wounds?

As for the girl's parents, the journey had come to a destructive end. They stopped at a tiny roadside motel late into the night to get some rest, and spoke to each other in whispers so as not to wake the young girl they now feared.

"I thought maybe Abuela was speaking through Floramaria, or perhaps God. I was scared but also proud that maybe my daughter was a prophet, but no. She has only caused pain. And if the Lord has not led her down this path, given her this information, then who else could it be but Satan himself?"

"My daughter is not evil."

"Nor is my God."

"Perhaps she will grow out of this."

"And if she doesn't?"

Neither seemed to know what to say. The room fell quiet for a few moments as the parents settled into sleep. Elizabeth alone remained alert and on watch. That is, until four familiar angels entered through the garishly painted walls to join her.

"We told you this was a bad idea," spat Alexis, the lead angel of their household. "What did you expect to happen?"

"Is true. Why you no listen?" Vlad asked in his heavy accent.

"I know it's hard to let go, but you've just gotta for her sake." Julio pointed to Floramaria sleeping soundly on the motel sofa. "For all of their sakes."

"She's not going to recover from this," Julio said with a sigh. "I can tell. It's one thing to hurt your own charge, but do you realize what you've done to each of ours? Bad things are coming."

"Yeah, and it's all your fault," Alexis huffed. "So, so selfish."

The angels, regrettably, were right about everything. Back at home, Floramaria's mother grew distant, having become fearful of her own child. Her brothers picked on the little girl, called her crazy for talking to ghosts, yelled at her for upsetting their mother. Only her father remained on Flora's side, yet he worked such long hours that he was never around to stick up for her.

Despite it all, Flora remained a happy and imaginative child, although she tended to keep mostly to herself. She often found herself alone, but never seemed to mind.

"Do you want to play?" she said to her dolly.

Elizabeth watched with interest as the girl and doll danced about the room in the most graceful of waltzes. "See, it's not so bad to be alone," she whispered to the girl. Even though she couldn't hold direct conversations with her charge, she still enjoyed talking to her the way one spoke to a treasured object or favorite pet.

"But I'm not alone," the girl murmured back. "You're always with me."

Elizabeth froze. Had Flora just answered her back? It was impossible. But then she remembered… Yes, this had happened before—at Theo's. Hadn't it? She'd never been able to communicate with her directly when she'd been Daisy, and it had been years since Flora had grown too old to see her any longer.

Still, she wanted to know for sure, so Elizabeth leaned in once more. "Do you know who I am?"

The little girl nodded. "You're my angel, and I love you."

Excitement overcame Elizabeth. Was this really, truly happening? Then to Floramaria, "How long have you known I was here?"

"Since the beginning."

"And you aren't afraid?"

"Why would I be afraid? You're here to keep me safe… right?"

"Right." The air around Elizabeth pulsed. None of this made any sense, yet here they were. Did this mean Floramaria had come to the cusp between her world and the next? Was another horrible step in the plan approaching?

Luckily, Floramaria did not seem privy to these thoughts that worried Elizabeth so. "You held me when I died the first time, and I held you when you died the last time. Do you remember?"

"Of course, I remember."

Flora smiled, but did not look happy. "You were my mom before."

"And now I'm your angel, which is even better."

"How can you be both my mom and my angel, and how can I be both Flora and Daisy? It's kind of confusing." She giggled, and Elizabeth joined in.

"You're right. It is confusing. Who you are is so much more than either Daisy or Flora. You aren't your body, you know. You're the soul inside it."

"But *you* don't have a body."

"I don't have one anymore. I did once. If you can't see me, then how do you know I'm here?"

"I can feel you with me always, but I can kind of see you, too."

"Even though I don't have a body?"

"I know where you are, because..." She chewed on her lower lip. "Well, because I just do. The air looks different where you are. More shiny, I think."

Elizabeth thought about this for a moment. She saw the other angels in human form, but she doubted that was what they really looked like, whether they actually had a set appearance or if their images—and her own—were decided by those who looked upon them.

Daisy picked up her brush and began to run it through her doll's beautiful blonde hair, such a contrast to her own dark locks. "Why are you here with me?"

Elizabeth didn't need to think about this one. There was only one answer, had only ever been one. "To protect you."

"And why am I here?"

"That's a really good question, one people much older than you don't have the answer to, and often don't even think to ask."

"That's not really an answer. Do you not know?"

Elizabeth realized she had figured out the answer as she watched those she loved from afar. She'd known ever since she first laid eyes on Daisy, and she knew it now standing here with Floramaria, too. "I've thought about it a long time. If you ask me, the meaning of life is love."

"I figured," the little girl said, then returned to dancing with her doll.

PART VIII

Elizabeth seemed to be the only one who liked spending any time with Floramaria at all. The more the girl spoke of her past life as Daisy, the more her family—especially her mother—grew to fear her.

"Why don't you just put the memories aside? Make new ones?" Elizabeth asked her one day, but Flora refused to hear it.

"They're part of who I am. You don't just turn your back on what makes you *you.*"

And truly the girl was wise, although not always intelligent. She soon took to carrying out her conversations with the angel no matter who else was around to hear them. One day, a teacher referred Floramaria to the school guidance counselor.

Her parents were called in to discuss Flora's *special needs.*

"You see," the counselor said, steepling his fingers and tapping them against his chin. "Floramaria's a very... special... girl, and she'll need some extra attention in order to excel in the classroom. I believe she may be schizophrenic. She's calm enough now, but if she were to have an outburst and hurt one of the other children..."

"We understand," her father said. His shoulders slumped, his spine curved in. If he'd had a tail, it would surely have gone between his legs.

"The district's special education program is one of the leading programs in the state. Floramaria will be in very capable hands."

The girl's mother sobbed and hid her face behind her palms. A charged silence settled between them, and finally the parents left murmuring their thanks and apologies.

That was when Peter appeared to Elizabeth.

"You have done so much harm here." He shook his head sorrowfully. "There will be consequences. This is only the first of many."

He snapped his fingers and they appeared together in Floramaria's bedroom.

"Hi, Elizabeth," the girl said with a big grin. She either didn't sense or didn't acknowledge the other angel.

Peter gestured toward the girl. "You should tell her. It will be better coming from you."

Flora turned a page in her book, oblivious to Peter's presence. She looked so happy, so at peace. Was her life really about to turn upside down all because of Elizabeth's inability to let go of their shared past? Still, she enjoyed their talks, liked being an active part of the girl's life rather than simply an invisible observer. How much harm would really be done if…?

"Quit stalling," Peter said. "Her parents will be home soon. Would you prefer she heard it from them?"

"Darling, there's something you need to know," Elizabeth began. Then to Peter, "How do I tell her?"

"Tell her the truth. That's all anyone ever needs."

"But the plan…?"

"Isn't set yet. She needs to claim her power to decide while it's still available to her."

Flora set her book aside. "Is everything all right?"

"Not exactly." Elizabeth paused. Peter had mentioned consequences. Would they be for her or for Floramaria? Too late she realized that he had been right about everything. She'd taken away the girl's power over her own life. She'd held on too tight and had strangled Flora's autonomy. She gulped, then continued. Perhaps if she just focused on the facts, she could get through this.

"Life is about to get much more difficult for you, dear one. They say there's something wrong with you, even though there's not. If you were to just stop talking to me, then—"

"No!" The words came out loud and fierce, catching Elizabeth off guard. "You're my best friend. I love you."

Elizabeth's voice caught in her throat. "I love you too, Flora, but…"

"Then what is there to question? You're the only one I need, the only one I've ever needed."

Why was she fighting this? Couldn't she see that Elizabeth was trying to do the right thing here? Trying at last to put her own needs aside and focus only on what would be best for Flora? "You need other people too. You can't just depend on me for everything."

"Why not? You're the one who is always here when I need a friend. When I'm with you, I feel happy. Other people make me feel sad. Isn't it better to always feel happy?"

Peter placed a hand on her shoulder. "She doesn't want it. It's too late."

She shoved him aside. Why had he forced this confrontation if he knew it wasn't going to accomplish anything?

"Flora, don't you understand?" Elizabeth cried. "I can still be here for you, still protect you, from the background. If you'd just put some distance between us, your life could be so much easier."

The girl shook her head slowly. "I need you. You're the only one I need. I can't let you go."

"Okay," Elizabeth said. "Get back to your reading." She turned to ask Peter what would happen next, why he'd guilted her into this talk that he must have known wouldn't lead anywhere, but he had already disappeared, as if into thin air.

Flora grew to despise school, a bright girl forced into remedial classes. When finally she graduated, she refused to even consider the prospect of attending college.

"Why bother?" she said. "After all, it's not like my parents will pay for it."

And she was very right about that, for, on her eighteenth birthday, her parents served her an eviction notice, visibly relieved to finally be rid of their embarrassing and haunting burden.

Flora took it all in stride. "They'll be much happier without me around, and frankly I'll be happier without them too."

She went out and interviewed for a job as a cashier at the local super store, and the conversation with the hiring manager went well, until…

"Any history with substance abuse or mental illness?" He raised an eyebrow at her as if it were so very ridiculous that he'd even have to ask this question.

"Yes," she said pertly. "I've been diagnosed with schizophrenia."

His eyes bulged. He adjusted his tie and shifted his gaze to the floor.

"But I don't have it," she assured him.

"The diagnosis was overturned?" A relieved smile spread from cheek to chubby cheek.

"No, they only think I have it because I talk to my angel."

"You speak with… with angels?"

"Just one angel. Her name is Elizabeth."

He scrambled to his feet, knocking the clipboard and pen to the floor. Reaching his hand out to Flora, he sputtered, "Th—thank you very much for your time."

He scuttled away, and Flora burst into giggles.

"What was that about?" Elizabeth asked, not sure if she was more confused or angry.

Flora shrugged. "I didn't want that job anyway. Did you see how unhappy all the cashiers looked? The greeters too."

"But, Flora!" Elizabeth protested. "You need a job. That's part of life!"

"Why? Because it's expected? You know very well I've never done what's expected."

She had a point. What she didn't have was a job, a home, or any prospects for either. Luckily, she didn't seem to mind much, if at all.

Ultimately, they found themselves taking up residence in the local homeless shelter. Flora continued to do things her own way even if others began to systematically avoid her as a result. After all, the only thing worse than a homeless lady was a *crazy* homeless lady—and as far as anyone knew, Floramaria fit the part perfectly.

Although she pretended it didn't bother her, Elizabeth knew the girl must be lonely for some earthly company or that she at least needed a break every now and then from their prying eyes and furrowed brows. Every evening, Floramaria would take a walk through the city. She said she liked watching the sparkling lights of commerce come to life in the darkened sky, but Elizabeth knew their nocturnal adventures were more about privacy than anything else. It was at these times that they'd have their deepest conversations.

"What's it like in Heaven?" she asked one evening. It was not the first time the topic had come up, but Elizabeth's answer never seemed to give her what she needed.

"White. Big. Warm."

"Is that all? It seems you'd have a lot more to say about Heaven."

"Well, I've never actually been inside, just near it. For all I know it's completely different on the other side of the Gates."

"Okay then, what do you *think* it's like?"

Elizabeth mulled this over as she and her charge drifted through the urban nightscape. "I think it would be bright like the sun, and soft like a fleece blanket, and…"

A woman rushed by hugging a rich fur coat tight to her chest and crossed to the other side of the street to avoid them, but not before shooting Flora a dirty glance.

"Doesn't it bother you, how other people react to seeing you?" Elizabeth asked, watching as the woman's patent red heels clicked down an adjacent alleyway.

"Nope, I got used to it a long time ago. Anyway, Heaven—"

A scream raced toward them through the dark air. Elizabeth immediately knew it must belong to the woman they'd just passed.

"Run, Flora. It's not safe here," she commanded.

"No, she needs my help." Flora said with a determination Elizabeth hadn't often seen in her.

Elizabeth watched helplessly as the girl raced down the alley where she found the woman pressed up against the dumpster by a man holding a knife in his teeth. His hands clawed at her dress. Her beautiful fur coat was tossed in a nearby puddle, the contents of her purse scattered across the pavement.

The man glowered at Floramaria. "You want to be next in line, sweetie?" he growled, then pressed his mouth to the woman's exposed breast.

"L-leave her alone," Flora's voice shook, but she stayed rooted in place.

"So you wanna be first, huh?" He sniggered and reached out to grab Flora while keeping one hand clamped to the wrist of his other victim.

He was fast, but Elizabeth was faster. She reached toward Flora's arm and used it to deftly grab the man's knife from between his teeth. With one more sharp, fluid motion, she leaned in close and pressed the blade to his Adam's apple. Elizabeth had never been so thankful for the dodge ability, neither in this life nor the last.

He raised his hands above his shoulders and tried to take a step back, but Flora was ready for any attempts toward making an escape.

"Hey, hun. Calm down, all right? I was just having a little fun."

"Call the cops," Flora shouted to the woman who had already leaned down to retrieve her cell phone from the pavement.

"Take my coat," she ordered after the call had been placed, carefully shrugging out of one sleeve at a time. The woman's coat was covered in rain water and her dress was torn, exposing her naked upper body.

A few minutes later the police arrived and Flora slipped away into the night as the other woman recounted the details of the attack and the officers cuffed their new prisoner.

"Weren't you scared?" Elizabeth asked as the scene replayed again and again before her eyes.

"Kind of, but what's there to be scared of when I know there's life after death? That woman needed me, and I was in a position to help, so I did. And you know what else? I feel like finally I have a reason for being here more than just getting in everyone's way, like I can make a difference, do some good for others, the way you do for me." They made it back to the shelter, and Flora sank into an open bunk.

As she lay their waiting for sleep, she confessed, "You know what? I was actually a little scared, but it was weird. I had this déjà vu feeling of having sex when I didn't want it. I was afraid he'd hit me, hurt the baby. Was that…was that Victor?"

Elizabeth shuddered at the memory. "Yes, he was not good to you."

"Well, hopefully they'll put this other guy behind bars for a long time. Good night, Elizabeth."

"Good night, darling."

"Hey, hey, Miss. Is this you?" A man wearing mismatched boots and a red skull cap shook

Floramaria awake and shoved a crinkled newspaper in her face. A picture from a grainy security camera clearly showed Flora holding a knife to the would-be rapist's neck while the woman clenched Flora's jacket around her shoulders.

She rubbed the sleep from her eyes and snatched the paper for a closer look. "Do-gooder hobo saves hotel heiress from crime," she read aloud.

"Yeah, that's me," she said to the man who still lingered, a huge smile upon his dirty face. "Mind if I borrow this?"

He bobbed his head and then crossed the room back to his own bunk.

"The do-gooder hobo," Flora read again, then chuckled. "It's like my very own superhero name. I like it!"

"Well, I'm glad you're amused," Elizabeth said. "Because you put yourself in real danger last night."

"No, I was never in any danger. Not with you there to protect me. And, look, we saved that woman from whatever that guy's filthy intentions were. We could save more women, more people, live up to my new name. What do you think?"

"Frankly," Elizabeth paused, "I think you're nuts."

"Well, that makes you and everyone else. C'mon, Elizabeth. We have the chance to do real good here.

We can make a difference in people's lives. I can be a protector, just like you. Remember what I said last night? This feels like my purpose. I finally found something to live for. Don't take that away from me, Elizabeth, please."

The angel sighed in resignation. "Seems you've already made up your mind."

Flora nodded and smiled. She knew Elizabeth would ultimately support Flora in whatever decisions she made, whether or not they seemed entirely rational.

"When did you become so stubborn?" Although she was definitely annoyed, Elizabeth also swelled with pride. Perhaps she hadn't ruined things for her charge after all.

Before Flora could answer, a couple wearing sleek expensive-looking suits marched into the shelter. They scanned the large room filled with mismatched furniture before spotting Flora and striding over to say hello.

"It's you," the woman said—the same woman from last night. "You saved me. How can I ever thank you enough?"

Flora stood and allowed the woman to wrap her in a hug. She didn't seem to mind that Flora hadn't showered for nearly a week, nor that her dark hair was completely overwhelmed by tangles.

"I'm just glad you're okay," Floramaria said.

"I'm more than okay, thanks to you. And, look." She gestured to the newspaper. "The city is finally taking street crime more seriously now that this has happened. There's even a new bill starting its rounds over at city hall. It would make things so much safer for all of us."

"That's good," Flora said with a laugh. "Seeing as the streets are where I live."

The woman frowned. "They don't have to be. Come home with me. Let me give you a warm meal, a hot shower, and a clean pair of clothes. I could take care of you, help you get back on your feet."

Flora shook her head. "That's okay. I'm happy right where I am."

"But how could you possibly—?"

"I have everything I need, and now I have the opportunity to help protect others too."

They both fell silent.

"Actually there is one thing you could do for me," Flora said at last.

"Anything. Name your price." The woman reached into her pocketbook and extracted a wad of cash.

"Keep your money. But that new legislation you mentioned that would help keep people safe? Please make sure it passes."

"Yes, yes, of course," the woman said, gave Flora another quick hug and a business card with her number on it, then left.

"So what next?" Elizabeth asked once the couple had gone.

"Isn't that obvious? Next we make a difference in people's lives. We do what we were put here to do. It's not just *my* purpose. It's ours."

"Is that all?"

"Well, at least it's a start. Let's see what happens after that."

Elizabeth hoped Peter would forgive her interference in Flora's life when he heard of this latest development. He'd mentioned consequences, and she was pretty sure she hadn't seen the last of them… nor had Floramaria.

PART IX

Elizabeth suspected that maybe—just maybe—all the others had been right about Floramaria. Maybe she *was* crazy, at least just a little bit. After all, who else would choose to remain homeless when given any other option? Still, the angel couldn't deny the happiness this unique "work" brought to her charge.

As each *thank you* spilled forth from yet another pair of lips, Flora's own smile became wider and wider. As did Elizabeth's.

"I'm just happy I was here to help," she'd say. "God isn't done with you yet. You have a purpose."

Flora's goodness and profession of God's plan led some to label her a prophet. Christians, Jews, Muslims, Hindus, even Wiccans, would seek the girl out, hoping to snag a little bit of her other-worldly wisdom. They asked her to lay hands upon them, to bless them, even to heal them of impossible wounds and illness.

"I'm nobody special," Flora would say, shaking her head. "I'm just doing the best I can while I'm here. I hope that you'll find your peace."

And even though she couldn't exercise powers she didn't have nor would she pledge herself to any organized faith, her visitors left happy, relaxed, *changed.*

"Aren't you tired? Sore? Hungry?" Elizabeth would often ask as she and Flora took yet another long trip through the city, moving along from sunup to sundown with hardly a scrap to eat.

"Mind over matter." Flora tapped her head in response. "I don't have to be any of those things if I choose not to acknowledge them."

This was all part of the reason, Elizabeth supposed, that Flora's nickname had evolved from the Do-Gooder Hobo to the Homeless Prophet. Some even suspected that she was the latest incarnation of history's famous Wandering Jew.

That made Flora laugh. "Why can't people just let me be *me*? Why does everything have to mean so much to them? You see it, don't you? That's the whole problem with the world these days. That everything *needs* to be important. Nothing can just *be*."

"How did you get so smart?" Elizabeth asked her charge. Wasn't it she who should be imparting such wisdom rather than the other way around?

"I think..." Daisy stopped walking and tapped her chin pensively. "Well, I think we are all born with everything we already need to know. Most people grow up, get distracted, and stop listening to the voice of their heart." She smiled. "That voice is you, Elizabeth."

If her visitors thought anything of Flora holding regular conversations with her invisible angel, they didn't let on. Probably assumed she was speaking with the heavenly father rather than her celestial mother.

Elizabeth still *felt* like a woman although she hadn't occupied a body in almost sixty years. She wondered if it was the same for God. Was God truly a man? Had he ever been, or was it just easier to assign human traits to the divine in a desperate attempt to understand the unknowable?

Flora's apostles—as the frequent visitors called themselves—had learned her daily route and often stopped in to offer fresh bottles of juice and leftovers from their kitchens. Whenever they brought money, Flora would decline it, telling them instead to find a cause they believed in and give their money there.

"Don't depend on me to make a difference," she'd say. "Go and make it yourself."

Scholars came to study her, journalists came to interview her, and seekers came to know her. Flora enjoyed the constant stream of company even though she refused to acknowledge their assertions that she was something more than mortal. In fact, she listened far more than she spoke, meaning—if anything—she was closer to a therapist than a spiritual leader.

She listened to Elizabeth, too. Well, she heard her words at least.

Over the years, Elizabeth felt more and more loved by her charge, though less and less needed. Flora's reflexes were quick, her body lithe, her heart pure. Elizabeth so rarely got to use her abilities that it sometimes took her a moment to remember that she still could help in those special moments when Flora still needed her.

Like today.

They were weaving their second loop through the city that day when Flora's threadbare boot snagged the curb and sent her hurtling out into traffic.

Elizabeth leaped forward into Flora's body and dodged with all her might. The move saved her from an oncoming bus, but also threw her hard into the concrete.

"That was way too close a call!" Elizabeth shouted as she hovered over her charge.

Normally, when the unexpected happened, Flora would smile, brush herself off, and continue on her path, but today she lingered on the pavement. She lay flat on her back as she took short, ragged breaths, her eyes closed to the sun.

"I'm sorry I hurt you, but it would have hurt a lot more if you'd gotten hit by that bus." Elizabeth laughed, trying to lighten the mood, but Flora did not join her.

Worry began to sink in.

"Flora? Flora? Is everything okay?"

The girl—now a middle-aged woman—opened her eyes and spoke softly to her angel. "Everything is fine. But I'm not sure I can get up."

"Oh, no! Did something break?"

"No." *Gasp.* "I'm just…" *Pant.* "Really tired."

Elizabeth searched Flora's head for bumps, but couldn't see any beneath her matted hair and did not have the luxury of touch.

"Flora, I think you may have a concussion. I'm sorry I threw you so hard. I should have been more gentle."

"It's not your fault." She smiled weakly. "Do you think you can use your dodge again to help me get back on my feet? We still have another few miles to go before sundown."

"I'll help, but only if you promise to go to the free clinic and get your head checked out."

"Elizabeth, I—"

"Promise me."

She let out a slow laugh and rolled her eyes. "Okay, I promise."

They sat in the clinic waiting room for what felt like forever—and Elizabeth knew all too well what *that* felt like—until finally the doctor ushered them back into one of the glaringly bright exam rooms.

"I've heard about you," she said while checking Flora's eyes with her light. "You're the Homeless Prophet, right?"

Flora shrugged. "That's what they call me."

"I've been following the stories about you for years. Big fan here." The doctor grinned, revealing a perfect, white smile, then lifted her stethoscope to her ears. "Look, your medical records are pretty sparse. Take a deep breath. I'd feel a lot better if you let me run a full physical. Would you mind humoring me a bit? Okay, let it out."

Flora looked uncomfortable, but agreed nonetheless. "Well, since I'm already here..."

"Another breath in… And out. Perfect. I'm going to send you down to the lab for a blood test. I'm guessing you don't have a phone, so can you swing back in a couple days for the results?"

"I can do that."

"Great. No concussion by the way, but still take it easy over the next few days. Can you do that for me?"

"No problem."

The doctor shocked them both by giving Flora a tight hug while they were on their way out. "I'm so glad I got to meet you," she gushed. "Well, I won't keep you any longer. But I'll see you in a couple days, okay?"

As they left, Elizabeth noticed the doctor had the hint of a tear at the corner of each eye.

When they returned to the clinic a couple days later, there was no waiting. The doctor immediately led them back to an exam room and sat Flora down.

Elizabeth's chest clenched when she noticed the faraway look in the woman's eyes.

"There's no easy way to say this," the doctor said, frowning at her chart. "Your results came back, and you have *c-cancer*." She choked on the word, though it must be one she'd said many times in the course of her work. Her eyes swept over Flora's body as if searching for an answer she couldn't find herself.

If Elizabeth had possessed a physical heart, it surely would have ached just then—to see the doctor so torn up about the diagnosis, to see no visible reaction from the woman who had just quite possibly been handed a death sentence.

There are so, so many ways to die, Elizabeth mused, wondering how many of them she'd experienced in her time as a mortal, how many of them she'd have to guide her charge through before her time was finally up.

After a moment, the doctor took a deep breath and continued. "Unfortunately, it's pretty advanced. We could start chemo right away, but…"

Flora nodded. "I understand. Thank you, doctor."

When the doctor left, Flora looked up toward the ceiling as she often did when talking with Elizabeth. "So I'm going to die. *Huh*."

Elizabeth ran over all the things she could say. She could promise Flora that, no, she wouldn't, that they would fight this thing, that everything would be fine, but her charge didn't seem to need any reassurance. *I'm going to die*—the words held no sadness, no anger, only a declaration of what was to be.

"I don't remember the last time I died, not anymore. What was it like? Does it hurt?"

The angel still well remembered Daisy's horrific death—the violent showdown with Victor, the slow drain of blood from the teen's womb until she'd lost too much to go on… And now she also saw the image of the little girl she'd always loved converge with the middle-aged woman before her—as Daisy, as Flora—so curious, so innocent, so vulnerable.

She'd miss being such an active part of her charge's life, but Elizabeth also knew that she'd need to stay in the background of Flora's next life for the girl's own good. How she would miss her.

"Elizabeth?" Flora asked when the angel failed to answer her. "Are you okay?"

"Yes, yes, everything will be fine, baby. Nothing to worry about." She shook her head like an etch-a-sketch, trying uselessly to wipe away the indelible images she so often found herself looking upon.

Pop! Peter appeared in the far corner of the room and motioned toward Elizabeth.

The angel sighed. Once again, Peter's timing was not the best, but she knew better than to argue with him. She turned to Flora and whispered, "You have a lot to think about. Let me give you a few moments to yourself. I'll be back soon, and then we can talk everything through."

Peter nodded, came forward, laid a hand upon her shoulder, and took them both away into a far-off place. Everything was white, though he hadn't brought her to the Gates. Snow, endless snow surrounded them.

Elizabeth shivered at the memory of how the frigid air had once pricked at her flesh.

The other angel studied her. "Do you know why I brought you here?" he asked.

"To talk about Flora, I'm guessing."

His gaze darted toward the earth, and he took a deep breath before continuing. "Yes."

"She's going to die, right? The plan…" She didn't know how to finish that thought, but luckily Peter didn't need her to.

His eyes locked on hers. "Yes."

"Will it be any easier this time?"

"No. It never gets easier watching the one you love die. *Never.*"

"Then what are we doing here? I should be with her."

Peter drew closer to her, so close she could almost feel him, though neither of them possessed a physical body. Then, as if he'd realized some mistake, he backed away even farther than before. "Patience. I'm trying to help."

"So then help."

Why did he always have to make her so angry? Why couldn't he just be direct from the get-go, save them both this annoying rigmarole?

He drew close again, excitement dancing in his eyes. "Flora has a real chance at becoming a Pearl after this life. It's so rare for it to happen with this few attempts, but as you know, she's lived quite the extraordinary existence."

Elizabeth chuckled softly, remembering all the times she'd shared with both Daisy and Floramaria. Would that be it? She felt excited for the possibility of passing through the Gates with her charge, but also terrified, as if she'd be losing something vital in the process.

Peter continued, "When you return, urge her to make all things right. As quickly as possible. She doesn't have much time."

"How do I do that?"

"Talk to her about her regrets, about anything she'd change if given the chance."

Elizabeth shook her head. "But Flora loves her life. She often says she wouldn't change a thing."

"Death has a funny way of bringing hidden sadness to light. Ask her again. You'll see."

Determination surged through the angel. She could do this, she would. Flora deserved it, and Elizabeth owed it to her. She shook her head.

"I will, but Peter?"

"Yes?" He hovered a few inches off the ground and a whirling blizzard of fresh snow passed through his form, creating a beautiful show of speckled light and shadows. And she realized then that she would miss him, that he'd been just as constant a companion as Flora. That he had become an important part of who she was, that she needed him in a way.

"If Flora does become a Pearl, she and I will both get to go to Heaven, right?"

"Right."

"What will happen to you?"

A range of emotions crossed his face—ebullience, fear, longing. He lowered himself to the ground and sat atop the fresh snow, not leaving an indent. "That, I don't know."

No one would ever know the angels had been there, and if Flora died without reaching the Gates, she too would soon forget Elizabeth. But if they did make it to Heaven, would she forget Peter, her mentor, her advisor, *her friend*?

The divine plan certainly came with a fair number of what-ifs. And what did Elizabeth want in the end?

All at once, everything felt less certain, but somehow so much more real.

PART X

Elizabeth came back into the tiny clinic waiting room and found Flora just as she'd left her, staring vacantly into space, her face an unreadable mask. She wasn't certain whether it was better to say something or give her charge more time to come to terms with her approaching death.

So she waited and thought over all that Peter had revealed in the wintery abyss. "Make things right," he'd said. "This might be it. She could make it. You could make it together."

She remained unconvinced, for Flora had lived a life filled with service and sacrifice. Didn't that mean she'd become a Protector, too? And, if it did, what would happen to Elizabeth?

"No, that won't happen," Peter had said flatly when she voiced her concerns.

"But think about it, if she—"

"It doesn't work like that," he snapped. Peter never snapped.

He turned away from her and seemed to shiver despite not being able to feel the cold.

"Just go to her. Help her resolve any unfinished business. Greet the end when it comes, and then we'll see what's what."

"*Elizabeth?*" the meek voice that called to her didn't belong to Peter.

Flora had finally decided it was time to talk.

"Yes, darling?" The moment had arrived. It was time to speak of Flora's life in the past tense, to make conjectures about what happened next, to urge her to make things right—as if anything were actually wrong. Would they go to Heaven together? Would they take on a new, more solitary set of lives? Would Flora become a Pearl and Elizabeth dissolve into nothingness?

So much rested on what happened next.

"We should go. They probably need this room for another patient."

The mundane pragmatism of that statement startled Elizabeth. Where was the earth-shattering epiphany? Where was the reflection, the emotion?

Surely, Flora had to be feeling something as she prepared to meet death head on.

"Go where?"

"It's too late to finish our loop today, so back to the shelter. We can start fresh tomorrow."

"Back to… the shelter? What about the hospital? What about chemo, or at least a comfortable bed to sleep in?"

Flora let out a sad chuckle. "No. Why should I change things just because I'm going to die? I like my life, and I plan to live the days I have left."

"But, Flora, you're sick! You're weak! You need—"

"I need to do this my way, Elizabeth. You know I love you, but this is something that *I* need to handle, and in a way that makes sense to *me*."

Elizabeth wouldn't make any ground this way, not with Flora being as stubborn as ever when it came to making even the slightest change in her routine.

Suddenly, an idea.

"Are you sure the shelter will be comfortable enough, though? Maybe we should consider going home."

Elizabeth paused, her spine straightened, and she spoke so softly Elizabeth almost couldn't hear her.

"Home."

"Yes, wouldn't it be nice to check in on your mother and brothers before...?" She let the implication linger as she watched Flora carefully for any signs of giving in.

"I haven't been there since Mama threw me out of Pop's funeral. Was that fifteen years ago? No." She began to walk again, faster now. "Home is the shelter. That's where I belong."

"But don't you want to say goodbye?"

"I want to be happy, Elizabeth. Don't you understand? Why would I want to go back there and be faced with my very worst memories in life? Why would I want to be reminded of how I failed as a daughter, and of how she failed me as a mother? No good can come of it, I promise you that."

"Maybe it still can. You could forgive her. Imagine how good it would feel to leave this life with no regrets."

Flora rounded her shoulders and focused her gaze straight ahead.

"No."

Well, now what was Elizabeth supposed to do?

Elizabeth needed to speak with Peter to get his advice when it came to managing Floramaria's unwillingness to visit—and forgive—her mother. But the other angel was strangely absent for the weeks that followed.

Elizabeth tried her best to convince Flora to set things right, but the more she brought up the topic, the more Flora began to shut her out. She was so weak these days that they couldn't even do one full loop of the city, let alone multiple rounds. Now they only walked a half dozen blocks from the shelter and spent the entire day seated at a fountain Flora had a particular fondness for.

They watched together as the water burst into the air then rained back into the shallow pool below. Pennies glinted just beneath the surface, wishes that still had the potential to come true. But what about Elizabeth's wish? What about her desire to cross through the Gates with her dear charge, to no longer face the constant uncertainty of life after life, failure after failure?

"Are you the Homeless Prophet?" A girl who appeared to be in her twenties came up to them.

Flora opened her mouth to speak, but seemed to find the effort too tiring. Instead, she nodded slightly and smiled wanly. She was weak, dying, and sitting out in the sun all day certainly didn't do her ailing body any favors.

"We've been studying you in sociology class. Could I… if it's not too much to ask, maybe have your autograph?" She rummaged in her pack and brought out an old style composition journal.

This, Elizabeth realized, was her last chance to do as Peter had told her. If Flora wouldn't go to her mother, perhaps Elizabeth could bring her mother here. Flora wouldn't listen to her suggestions, but could she fight off Elizabeth's dodge in her weakened state?

Flora gripped the pen the student handed her, and Elizabeth reached for it too by moving through Flora's fingers. She felt her charge relax into her, completely unaware of the betrayal Elizabeth had planned.

"It's for your own good," she whispered as she made a series of loopy letters in the notebook. By the time Flora realized what the angel had done, it was too late.

Please tell my mother I need to see her before I die. Have her meet me here tomorrow at the fountain. Her name is Anita, and she lives at 555 Sandy Springs Drive.

The girl's lips moved and she read over the note, then she flapped the journal closed and fixed a smile on poor, meek Floramaria.

"Yes, I will. I'll do whatever I can to help."

Flora was angry with Elizabeth, but she was also a

creature of habit. As planned, she awoke early and took the walk into town to wait by the fountain. Her feet dragged beneath her, and she had to take several breaks during the short trek, but she made it.

When they arrived, Anita was already waiting. She remained seated on a nearby bench and watched as Floramaria took the final steps to reach the fountain. She did not smile, but she also didn't look away. She just waited, as if she too needed this to happen.

She helped Flora to sit once she had reached the lip of the fountain, and even handed her a pair of pennies. It was a long time before either of them spoke, and, while Elizabeth was glad Anita had finally made an effort when it came to her daughter, she was also furious. How could this woman so carelessly and deliberately throw away the one thing Elizabeth gave her life to protect?

But this meeting wasn't about Elizabeth's anger; it was about Flora's—about making things right.

Finally, Anita cleared her throat and spoke, although she stared at the pennies she'd placed into Flora's palm rather than making eye contact. The words that came out were obviously rehearsed.

"If I had a wish to make, it would be that I hadn't let my fear come between us. But I have been following the stories about you in the paper and on the news, and I'm proud of the woman you've become. I like to think that maybe I had a small part in that." She smiled wistfully. "So actually I won't apologize, and I won't make a wish today, but I thought maybe you could borrow mine. That way you have two if you need them."

Flora nodded sadly. "I forgave you a long time ago, but I only just realized that now."

"Well… I won't intrude on your day any longer." Anita pinched her mouth into a tight line, then rose to her feet.

"Wait," Flora called before Anita could make it more than a few paces. She struggled to her feet with raspy, labored breaths.

Elizabeth marveled at how such a simple motion—one so easily taken for granted in the day to day—had become such a struggle, almost as if she'd somehow forgotten how.

At last, Flora closed the small distance between herself and the mother who hadn't wanted her. Tears threatened to spill, the first since they'd received the doctor's diagnosis.

Anita remained stuck in place, a monument to everything Elizabeth had never wanted to be, all she had worked so hard to mitigate for her charge.

"We won't see each other again," Flora whispered into the older woman's ear. "And I just thought it might be nice to say goodbye with a hug."

Anita stiffened but allowed Flora to wrap her arms around her.

And then Flora smiled, her eyes rolled back in her head, and she slumped toward the ground, giving Anita no choice but to strengthen her grip, to speak.

"Floramaria, *Floramaria*! Somebody help!" she cried.

But even before the familiar white expanse began to overtake the urban cityscape, Elizabeth knew that Flora had passed on. Perhaps for good this time.

Once again, the unyielding wall of white surrounded her like an embrace, absorbed her, became her. Nothing existed except for the vast blankness. She drifted through it, a mere ripple in the endless ocean. She had returned, but this time she was not alone.

As she drew near the spectacular gates for the third time, she spied a figure standing outside them.

Waiting.

For her.

And, there, just outside of the beautiful city made of sunrise, she came face to face with her charge for the first time *ever.* The girl who greeted her was both Daisy and Floramaria, the daughter she had lost and the best friend she had confided in. She had become Elizabeth's whole world, though the two had never formally met—not like this.

"Elizabeth," her daughter choked. "You're here."

She ran toward Elizabeth, for the burden of her illness had lifted, and wrapped the angel into a huge hug. So much the opposite of the one that had just taken place on Earth, this embrace held all the longing, all the love, all the moments that had passed between them.

"I love you," Elizabeth sobbed, and the tears spilled across her cheeks in rivulets. All at once, she realized that something major had changed. Not just having her girl here with her in the flesh, but *having flesh.*

Flora's arms around her generated warmth, her skin smelled of berries. Elizabeth had not known that before this. But now all her senses came flooding back into focus, which meant…

"We made it. Flora, we're here!"

The girl, who had not yet been to this place, smiled as she looked up at the two soaring gates that rose so high neither of them could see to the tops.

"Is this Heaven?"

"Heaven is just beyond those gates."

Peter materialized beside them. Did that mean he was safe from whatever came next? Would he get to go through with them?

She forced her eyes away from Flora and looked at Peter who was wearing an impossibly large grin, having taken a form he had not used before. His sandy hair and crisp green eyes framed the most handsome face she had ever laid eyes upon. For she *had* seen this man, many lifetimes ago.

"Mary, my love," he cried. "Do you know me?"

She nodded, too moved to speak. She did know him. Intimately. He had been her husband, her love, her soulmate, apparently—because now they were here together just outside Heaven's Gates.

And then he was at her side, picking her up and swinging her around in perfect, blissful circles. "I've waited almost two hundred years for this moment to come, but I knew it would. I knew it. So many times I wanted to… But none of that matters, you're here. *We're* here."

She kissed him to show him that she, too, remembered their life together, his sacrifice that had let her live on while he… "You were always with me. This whole time."

"Do you remember our wedding? It was 1826, Massachusetts. You wore your mother's lace gown, and I had one of those top hats that were so stylish at the time. We promised forever, in sickness and in health. But we were also bound in life and in death, it seems. I have loved you for so many lifetimes. And now we are reunited at last, standing together once more as we look out upon forever. I'm so happy I feel as if I could burst."

And, in that moment, Elizabeth wasn't sure whom she loved more—the one she had protected or the one who had protected her. Luckily, they had come to a place of infinite love. They just had to walk through those Gates.

She reached out to Peter at her left and Flora at her right and clasped hands with each of them. Together, they all took the first step into the eternity they had journeyed so far to find.

Heaven.

EXTENDED ENDING

So Elizabeth and crew went to Heaven, good stuff. But I know what you're thinking. You're wondering what happened to that charming fellow, Daniel (that's me), and probably also about what happened to Theo, Tina, Victor, Anita, and basically everyone else.

Am I right?

Well, allow me to fill you in. Yeah, I know you probably got used to Elizabeth telling this story, but here's the deal... You don't hear from people once they pass through the Gates. You'll see her again once *you* become a Pearl, but until then you'll just have to trust me that everyone over there is doing swell.

As for me, I have a pretty major decision to make. You see, Theo kind of did that whole die-in-sacrifice thing, which is great for him and definitely great for the one he died to save. But as for me? I'm kind of stuck.

Yeah, Peter chose to stick around and become his protector's protector, given the whole soulmate thing he had going on with Elizabeth.

Gross…

I guess it helps if I tell you that I first knew Theo as Rebecca, my little sister. I saved her from drowning, but—oops—drowned myself in the process. Well, when your charge becomes a protector herself, most angels step aside and move on. Clearly, Peter was a special case, and that's fine. I get it. For *him*. Not really an option for me, though.

Which means I have two choices left.

Behind Door A: Paradise. That's right, I can cross through the Gates now and live an eternity of perfect bliss. But bliss seems kind of boring. I want adventure!

Which means I'm probably going to open Door B and take a promotion. Did you know there are multiple levels of angelhood? Back in the day they were called choirs, but now we just call them the ranks.

Guardians—protectors and wardens both—are the lowest rank. Above them, you've got the seraphim and cherubs, all the way up to archangels. But I've got my eye on one post in particular. Rumor has it the Angel of Death gig may soon have an opening, and—boy—does that sound like fun! If things go down the way I think they will, I should have that job in no time…

Until then, I guess I'll wait and see. Maybe tell a few more stories of my own. But which story? Aww, nuts, another decision.

Hey, maybe *you* can help me with this one.

I could tell you all about Theo and Tina and the paths that led them to each other. It's kind of a fun love story, because there are three super important people in it: Theo and Tina, of course, but also Elizabeth. Oh, and Daisy, too!

Or I could tell you about that jerk, Victor, and all about his comeuppance. You think the Maker was just going to let him off the hook for killing his girlfriend? Yeah, right! He got saddled with a warden angel for that one, and—oh—she is going to make him pay in this life, and the next, and the next…

My personal favorite story, though? All the crazy things that are happening with the current Angel of Death and a certain woman who's caught his eye. Yeah, somehow it always comes back to love around here. Maybe one day I'll even find it for myself, but until then I can't wait to take my next adventure.

So tell me which story you want to hear by casting your vote at www.MelStorm.com/decide. Until I find out more about this possible job opening, I guess I can settle for being a muse. Later, gators!

PETER'S STORY

I first spotted Mary standing across the church courtyard, talking very seriously with Father McGovern. Her brow furrowed and she nodded intently as he spoke, then almost all at once a huge smile broke out across her face, transforming it entirely. I watched, enraptured, as her cheeks crinkled in merriment, her chest rose and fell with laughter, and her eyes shone.

Although I stood still, my innards were all but dancing. For that was the exact moment I knew I'd make Mary my wife.

And sure as the day is long, I did make Mary my wife. A few short months later, summer was in full swing and we took our nuptials inside the big city church with high ceilings and polished pews. She blushed beneath her veil as she took my hand and promised to love me forever. I, in turn, pledged my undying love and support, then lifted the thin draping of lace from her cheek and pressed a mostly chaste kiss to her lips.

That evening, we sealed our union, and I swear I saw Heaven looming before me, all brilliant whites and golds and pearl.

We were happy together—as happy as two people could be, given the hardships that surrounded us in our rural New England town, given how hard we had to labor to make a life. But we could do anything just as long as we were together. Our joined hands made for light work, and life was good.

I thought I only needed the two of us, that united we could conquer any challenge, secure the most perfect life. That is, until she became thick with child, and my bliss reached unprecedented heights.

What sphere exists above Heaven? For I found it in that moment when she pressed my palm to her belly and asked if I could feel our baby kick. Somehow I knew he would be a boy and that he'd be strong like me, handsome and gentle like his mother.

And, oh, what a doting father I was! I worked long hours in the fields to ensure that Mary wouldn't have to strain herself. After all, she had the most important job in the entire world. It was only fair that I picked up an extra few hours each night to make sure things kept running smoothly.

And each night she'd greet me with a fine cooked meal and a tall glass of milk and regale me with beautiful stories of how she imagined our tot's life would shape up.

"He'll be tall, of course. Very tall. And also exceptionally smart. I think he may become a merchant in the big city. Wouldn't that be perfect? I picture him there selling fine goods from China and India, having the most refined wears that people travel miles to see. Can't you see it, Peter?"

I loved hearing her stories, and I made up my mind to travel to the city myself— just as soon as I could to find a book of letters and some ink so to teach her to record all her wonderful tales and save them for such a time as our son could enjoy them.

I had planned to go the following week, only I never got the chance. One day I came in from the fields to find Mary upon the floor, clutching her abdomen in pain. She rocked back and forth and held tears back behind squinted eyes.

"Mary!" I cried and raced to her side. "What's wrong?"

"Something… doesn't… feel right," she managed between jagged breaths, and her eyes opened wide to catch mine, a look of desperation in them.

"Please tell me our baby will be okay," she whispered under her breath.

"Yes, of course, he will be!" I said in an instant. "We'll make sure of it." Although I hated to leave her, I needed to go out long enough to ask the neighbor to fetch the doctor. Our nearest was a good ten minutes walking swift, but somehow I managed to make it in hardly more than five.

The doctor came and delivered his decree. "The pregnancy will be a struggle, but all should be well. Keep her off her feet and in bed from sunup to sundown. The less she moves the better for both her and the child." Then turning to Mary, "Chin up, love. It will be all right in the end."

After a few more minutes of speaking with us both, he pulled me outside and said, "It's worse than I let on. You could lose them both. Prayers should help, I'd think, but there are no guarantees."

That had settled it. While I didn't want Mary to be afraid, I also didn't want to spend even a moment apart from her. So I hired a neighbor to mind the fields for a large portion of our crops, and we went from poor to poorer, but we were together and that was the most important thing.

Winter came, and it was a cold one. We had little to eat, but we got by. Snow came early and heavy, stacking up outside the windowpanes and howling at the doors. My Mary and I huddled close together by the dying embers of the fire as we did all we could to keep warm.

Then the pain returned to her belly. Her face grew waxen, and she struggled for breath. I looked at her rotund form and the frantic twitching from within and knew our child was well on his way—and in such a storm at that!

Now, of course, I didn't want to leave her, no, but the doctor had made it very clear that he would need to be present for the birth. Even still I debated ignoring his advice and tending to Mary's labor on my own. But as the hours passed, she became paler and paler, her cries of pain began to weaken, and I knew that I must risk leaving her in order to save her—to save them both.

So I bundled Mary by the fire and left her with a fresh basin of water and all the dry linens we had in the cabin, then set off to bring the deliverer. I rushed to the nearest neighbor yet again—realizing at this point that I owed him all I had, which wasn't much, but would have to be enough—and I borrowed his mare to ride to town and find the doctor.

Ice slickened the path and we had to take the journey slower than either of us had liked, but my steed and I made it to the doctor's home… and found that he was not within it.

Imagine my consternation then! My family, our future, our lives depended on finding this man, yet he had gone off wandering in a blizzard.

I kicked at a nearby embankment of snow and yelled curses into the white wind. That was when a small boy—no more than ten, I'd wager—ran out of his warm house and into the cold with me.

"Are you looking for the doctor?" his surprisingly shrill voice asked.

"Yes," I said and watched as the single syllable floated out on a puff of warm breath.

"He ain't here, Mister. But…" He leaned in close to me as if to share a secret. "I saw him go off toward the hills. Old man Smith's wife's is mad as a hatter, and folks say she needs a special kind of emergency brain treatment so as not to go around hurting her children and husband. Do you reckon that's true, Sir?"

"Thank you," I said, not bothering to answer his question. I'd heard the rumors about Florence Smith, but I didn't have the time to worry as to whether they were true. I needed to get to the doctor, even if that meant prying him from the clutches of a lunatic.

The horse and I took the winding trail up the hill, having to stride into the biting wind. We were not but halfway up when we found the doctor stranded in the snow. His horse lay in a deepening drift, obviously too injured to go on, though several miles lay between them going up or down the large hillock.

"Peter?" the doctor recognized me at once and scampered to his feet clumsily. His nose and cheeks were blue, making me wonder just how long he'd been secluded in the storm.

"Yes, it's me. Mary and the baby are in trouble. You have to go to them!" I shouted, though the two of us stood close together.

"These roads are too icy, the snow too thick for me to make it on foot, and my horse is injured."

I didn't have to think twice. "The horse can't carry us both, not in this storm. It's too difficult already. So you take him, go to Mary. He belongs to the Browns, but can keep warm in our barn while you tend to her."

"But what will become of you? Of my horse?"

"Come back for me when you're done. I'll try to make it into town on foot. I'll see if I can help get your horse there, too."

"God be with you," he said, then I helped him onto the horse's back and he rode back down the hill at a slow, shaky trot. I watched until both rider and horse disappeared on the horizon, and with all the snow descending from the heavens, it didn't take long.

The horse and I leaned against each other as we did our best to push through the enormous drifts, following a zigzag path with the most gradual incline. Every few steps we'd have to take a moment to recuperate before we could carry on. All the while I wondered about Mary, about my son. Was he in this world yet? Was she out of danger? Was the doctor cutting the cord? Was the baby taking his first drink of life? Was Mary relieved, scared, joyful, something else altogether?

Night fell, though I couldn't tell you how much time had passed in this never-ending day. The horse, to his credit, kept going as best he could, but he had much more meat on him than I did, a much thicker coat to keep him warm.

I lost the feeling in my toes first, then the tips of my fingers, my nose, my cheeks, my ears. The cold started at the outer perimeter of my body and worked its way inward. Still, I kept going, toward my wife, my son, our future.

It was going to be fine. It was going to be fine. I just needed to lie down for a moment and rest.

When I opened my eyes again, I was home, Mary and our son were there, too. The doctor had saved them then returned to save me, just as he'd promised. I was so very grateful in that moment, felt so very complete.

"He's beautiful, Mary," I whispered, then ran a hand over the child's dark tuft of hair.

Mary continued to watch our son lovingly, and our son fixed his eyes on me… then burst into a wail.

"It's all right, dear. It's all right, little one," Mary cooed and held him into her breast.

"Let me take him, Mary," I said.

But Mary ignored my request and continued to soothe the fussy infant.

"Mary, I can help. Give him here," I repeated.

"Hush, love. Hush. Papa will be home soon."

"Mary, I'm right here!" I shouted, unable to believe my ears. And in that moment my eyes also betrayed me, because the whiteness of the blizzard returned, creeping from the corners of my eyes until it filled the entire space. But it wasn't the snow, nor was it cold. I had come to a big, blank space without the faintest idea as to how I'd arrived there.

"Welcome to Heaven, Peter," a man's voice said from behind the expanse of white.

"Heaven? Have I…?"

"Died? Yes, Peter, you have."

"There must be a mistake. I need to get back to Mary, to our child."

"And so you shall. Your sacrifice has joined you more than matrimony ever could. Come, let me tell you about your new life as a protector."

ANGELS IN OUR LIVES

I don't have a name. At least, I've never needed one before. I am simply Emily's protector, Emily's angel. I joined up with Emily the moment she was born. My favorite memory will always be seeing her squished, red face as she emerged from her mother's womb.

Oh, how I loved her immediately.

People seem to have a difficult time understanding love—giving love. People were designed with a strong self-preservation instinct, and when it comes right down to it, most will put their own interests first, regardless of how much they "love" someone else.

Angels, though, were designed differently. We have no sense of self, no need to preserve, and only love for the human race. We especially love *our* people.

Emily is my person, and I love her more than even the most enlightened human is capable of understanding.

That is why watching her right now is so difficult.

A paramedic pulls her limp body from the back seat of the car. Shards of glass from the rear windshield cover the street—a deadly dusting of snow.

Emily's mother stands to the side of the road sobbing into her hands. "I don't know what happened. I just lost control."

The officer standing beside her nods his head in sympathy.

I know what happened. I saw it all coming, and I wanted so desperately to stop it. But that was not the plan. Sometimes, bad things—horrible things—must happen to people to help them grow, to help them become Pearls.

I so badly want for Emily to become a Pearl. Because when she becomes one, I will too—and we will run and jump and play together on endless streets of gold. Although she's never met me, she will know me, and we will be perfect friends for eternity.

But that will come much later.

Emily doesn't know it yet, but she won't be able to run or jump or play—not with me or anyone else. The accident damaged her spine, which will make things tricky.

The air is frigid on this icy December night. I hover near Emily, doing my best to keep her temperature up.

One eye blinks open, then the other.

"She's awake!" shouts the paramedic taking her pulse. Soon a crowd has gathered around her stretcher.

Emily smiles weakly. She is such a brave little girl.

Her mother tiptoes closer. I wish I could tell her not to feel guilty, but that's something Mother's angel must work out with her. I am here for Emily. She is my only priority.

"Mama," Emily sputters, reaching forward. Her face twists in confusion when she can't sit up. She jerks and tries again—fails again. A scream rips through her, sending her mother to a heap on the ground.

"What's wrong?" she shrieks. "What did I do to my baby?"

"We won't know for sure until we get her to the hospital. Would you like to sit in back with her?" the same paramedic asks.

Mother nods, and we are off.

At the hospital, the doctor says what I already knew, what I knew even before it happened. "I'm so sorry,

Mrs. Bloom, but chances are Emily won't be able to walk again." He pauses and fixes his eyes on Mother, a mask of sympathy plastered to his otherwise haggard face.

The seconds tick by. Everyone looks at the floor rather than at each other.

When Emily's parents fail to say anything, the doctor clears his throat and continues. "She's very lucky that the damage is contained to the spinal region. She, otherwise, suffered no—"

"Lucky?" Mother demands. "Lucky would have been not having the accident. Lucky would have been this happening to me instead of my innocent little girl."

Emily's father, who met up with us at the hospital, strokes Mother's arm, but little can be done to soothe her.

The doctor bows his head and exits without saying anything further.

The room is still, but noisy nonetheless. A cacophony of beeps, ticks, and mechanical whirs swirl in the air above Emily's bed.

Her soft voice rises, struggling to be heard amidst the off-canter song of the healing implements. "I feel…" She trails off, then starts again. "Mama, why can't I…?"

It's just as well that Emily doesn't know how to ask this question, because her mother doesn't know how to answer.

The hum and buzz fades into the background. All anyone can hear is the lingering question, the one no one is willing to voice an answer to.

I wrap my invisible wings around my little girl and stroke her cheek until she falls into a deep slumber.

Emily drops her arms to the side and grips the wheels until her clenched fists turn white. She grunts, strains, and rocks her body from side to side. "It's no use," she groans.

"You can do this. Just try your best, and it will happen." Emily's mother has finally found her voice, but she has also found the misfortune of never saying the right thing at the right time.

"I *am* trying my best, and I still can't do it!" Emily slumps back into the chair, her face already drenched with tears.

"C'mon, we still have ten more minutes of physical therapy before we can take a rest." Mother places a hand on Emily's shoulder, but Emily shrinks away in disgust.

"No. Just leave me alone."

I linger until she stops crying. I've never been able to leave Emily by herself when there are tears. Eventually, she angles her chair toward the nightstand and grabs Fiona, her favorite dolly, from its surface. She uses a miniature brush to stroke the doll's golden hair, working herself into a trance. When she's brushing Fiona's hair, the rest of the world fades away. She's just an ordinary little girl with ordinary dreams and ordinary struggles. In this special world, she doesn't need a wheelchair to get around. She is just like everybody else.

I hate to do it, but I have to leave her now.

She needs me in a different way this time, and the very reason for my existence is to help her through life—especially times like these.

The walls are tight around me, an unwelcome change from my usual freedom. I stand and do a couple small laps around my enclosure before falling down, exhausted. If all goes according to plan, it shouldn't be too much longer now. My eyelids droop, and I allow myself a quick nap.

Mother's voice rouses me. "*Ooh*, look, Emmie. This one is so fluffy!"

Emily presses a hand to the glass and glances at me while stifling a yawn. It's strange feeling her vision fall on me—this is the first time it's ever happened.

My tail thumps a merry beat, and my tongue lolls from the side of my mouth. "Emily," I say, but it comes out as "Ruff!" Our eyes connect, and for the briefest of moments, I feel as if she's recognized me.

A small smile works its way out from the corners of her pinched mouth. "I like this one," she declares.

The store clerk lifts me from my display box and places me on Emily's lap. "She's a golden retriever. Just came in this morning. You're very lucky, because the goldens never last long around here."

Father asks a series of questions about how to best care for me and follows the clerk around with a shopping cart, adding toys I might like, the healthiest brand of food, a soft, pink bed.

I snuggle into Emily's warmth as she combs her fingers through my yellow fur. It feels so nice to be close to her like this. I could lose myself forever in this perfect, blissful moment.

"Are you sure this is the one you want?" Mother asks with a knowing smile.

"Yes, Lulu is my new best friend already."

A name. I finally have a name.

Life is different as Lulu, mostly for the better. Now, Emily can hug me back. She can talk to me, smile at me, love me the way I have always loved her.

And I am her best friend. I see it in the way she cares for me, in the way she whispers her deepest secrets into my oversized ears.

Although it's a challenge for her, Emily insists on being the one to feed me my breakfast and dinner. Twice a day she rolls over to the large pantry in the kitchen and reaches into the big bag her mother has positioned at just the right height. Using a small shovel, she measures out my meals, and often sneaks in extra when no one else is looking. She keeps constant watch over my water dish, and when the water level sinks too low, she grabs a big cup, fills it up at the bathroom sink, and pours a fresh supply into my bowl.

"Lulu's given her a reason to keep going," Father says to Mother one night after Emily's gone to bed. "All of a sudden, she's decided to try."

Mother grimaces. She wants to be Emily's savior—or, at least, not to *be* the reason her daughter needs saving.

I tiptoe away from them and use my cold, wet nose to push open Emily's door. I'm supposed to sleep downstairs in my bed, but I could never be comfortable away from my little girl. Although I try to be quiet, I'm still a bit too clumsy to make it up on the bed by myself. The comforter bunches under my paws and I fall to the floor with a thud.

"Lulu," she whispers, reaching down to stroke my head. "Good girl. C'mon."

And her encouragement is all I need to master the leap, landing on the mattress with a grace I didn't know I possessed.

She wraps her arms around me, pulling me close to her chest. Sleep comes easily.

Soon, the time comes for Emily to return to school. My days used to be full of love and play and cuddling, but now I must spend them glued to the front door waiting for my little girl to return. As an angel, I could follow her wherever she went. My corporeal form, however, does come with some drawbacks, and this is the biggest one.

After what feels like an eternity, the front door bursts open. Mother steps on my tail and hisses at me to "step aside."

Something is wrong.

Emily wheels past me without saying hello. She snorts, trying to hold back her sobs, but I can tell she's absolutely distraught.

"Don't cry, little one. It will all be okay," I say, which translates into "Woof, woof. Yip. Ruff!"

She looks up, her eyes a scratchy red. "Lulu."

I walk to her side, and she buries her hands in my fur. I will her to tell me what happened so that I know how to comfort her. Luckily, it works.

"Rachel says she doesn't want to sit next to me anymore, because she's worried she'll catch crippled. Then no one wanted to play at recess, and it was just such a terrible day." She sniffles and looks at me, a smile creeping across her face.

I use my big, flappy tongue to lick the tears from her face, and she giggles.

"But you'll still play with me. Won't you, girl? You're not like mean old Rachel. You're my very best friend."

Yes, I am. And I will be forever. She wipes at her tears as I retrieve our favorite tennis ball and place it on her lap. A robust game of fetch ensues.

In the weeks that follow, her classmates slowly remember what makes Emily *Emily*—her goofy smile, gentle heart, loving nature. Rachel still doesn't want to sit next to her, but now Emily has made a new friend, Julie, a new girl who just moved in from out of state. Julie talks with a slight stutter, but Emily is quick to confront anyone who mentions it, which means the two are mostly left alone. Quite a pair they make, but Emily claims I will always be her very best friend no matter what.

We've developed a routine. The repetition of our daily interactions seems to help Emily feel normal, and feeling normal is what little girls stymied by differentness need most of all.

Each morning, I wake her a few minutes before Mother comes into the room. I scoot down the bed on my belly and lick her toes. Even though her toes don't get much use these days, they still deserve love—and I am the one to give it to them, each and every morning.

After a few licks on her feet, I move up to her hands. That usually wakes her, but when it doesn't, I drag my tongue across her cheek, and she's up like a lightning bolt. We sneak in a few cuddles, and then Emily pretends to be asleep so that Mother can believe she is the one waking her gently each day.

The sun peeks through the blinds, alerting me to the time. I creep across the bed and begin our morning ritual. After a few quick licks on each foot, I am about to move up to Emily's hands, but something unexpected stops me in my tracks. It was so quick and so subtle, I almost decide to ignore it as a trick of the eye. But then it happens again.

A twitch. Emily's foot. It moved. Not much, but it moved!

I lick her more this time with vigor, and she giggles in a half-conscious state.

"Lulu, that tickles." I bark and continue my effort.

Mother rushes into the room at the sound of my call, and Emily sits up in bed. Both are just in time to notice the third twitch.

"Oh, Emmie!" Mother cries. "Look! You're moving all on your own!"

"Does this mean I can walk again?" my little girl asks. Her expression is filled to the brim with hope.

"I don't know, but I'd say it's a very good sign." Mother picks Emily up, and together the two swing about the room. Both are crying tears of joy.

The doctor tells us Emily is on the verge of a miracle, but that it will require patience and hard work to get her all the way there. She increases her physical therapy visits to three times per week, which means I'm often alone at home for the entire day. Still, I do not care. I use this time to rest up, so that I can support Emily extra whenever she is at home with me.

After all, I need every bit of help I can get when it comes to taking care of Emily. We each have to play our parts to make sure she gets her miracle.

Several months after the first twitch, another comes. This time, it's Emily's leg. Her entire body is regaining strength from the bottom up. The progress is slow and comes in bits and spurts, but Emily's spirits remain high. She is such a determined little girl. She is also growing by the day, and soon she will be bigger than me—but that doesn't lessen my love for her one bit.

Today, Mother brings home a new red toy for me to play with. It's big with handles on both sides, and it's very nice to chew.

"Here, girl," Emily calls, transitioning herself from her chair to the couch.

I run over, panting so hard from my excitement that I can barely breathe.

"Get the toy," she urges.

I drop it in her lap, and she invites me to take one of the handles in my mouth so that we can play some tug.

Emily pulls hard. She's strong from years of pushing herself around in that chair, but still I am stronger.

I *grr* and growl theatrically to make the game more fun.

Emily laughs and tugs so hard my paws drag across the carpet and into the couch. She's so much stronger than last time we played, so I decide to put all my strength into our game too.

I grit my teeth around the toy, grind my heels into the floor, and pull as hard as I can. Expecting the sudden weightlessness that comes with victory, I am shocked when Emily doesn't let go.

Instead, she holds on tight with her right hand and pushes into the couch with her left. Moments later she is standing. She is standing. *She is standing!*

As soon as she realizes what has happened, the shock causes her to fall straight back onto the floor.

Mother rushes in, a concerned look on her face.

But Emily is smiling through a blur of tears, pushing down on her palms, and slowly rising again.

Emily and I continue to play, and our games become better as her mobility improves. In the span of just a few years, she's progressed from her chair to a cane. Now, she is finally ready to graduate from both. She has gotten her miracle—just like I always knew she would.

Today is a special day. We are having a funeral for Jessie, which is what Emily chose to name her cane. Everyone is here to say their goodbyes—Mother, Father, Emily, Julie, me, even Paul, a new boy who just moved into the big house down the street.

Emily lowers what used to be her third leg into the hole she dug prior to the gathering. She insists on doing everything herself now that she is able. "We're here to commemorate the life and work of Jessie," Emily drawls as Julie and Mother pretend to weep.

"While I can't say I'll miss her. I appreciated her while she was here. Rest in peace, Jessie." Everyone mumbles "Rest in peace, Jessie" as they shovel dirt into the hole and the worn plastic stick disappears into the fresh earth.

Once everyone has adequately said their goodbyes, Julie jets off to her after school job and Emily's parents go inside to watch their favorite Thursday night TV show. This leaves just me, Emily, and Paul together outside.

Emily takes a seat on the garden bench and motions for me to lie at her feet.

Lowering myself to the ground has become a more difficult task than it once was—Emily's grown stronger as I have grown more fragile—but I ignore my bones' protests and curl up beside Emily near our favorite bed of irises.

Paul stands close by as he and Emily chat about their classes and friends at school. Emily is in eighth grade now, which means we have been together for more than six whole *wonderful* years. Emily's eyes hold a special sparkle, a look I would recognize anywhere. She is in love, and Paul is the object of her affection. I've had an inkling of her crush ever since Paul first wandered into our yard to ask Emily for help finding his way around the school on his first day. They became fast friends after that.

Sure enough, moments later she shifts their discussion to the topic of the upcoming Sadie Hawkins

Dance at their school. "It's next week, you know," she explains, tossing her companion a smile. "And I just thought it might be nice for the two of us to go together."

Paul stiffens, the air takes on a bitter scent, and I can tell he is about to break Emily's heart. I scramble to my feet as fast as I can, but I am too slow.

"I don't really think of you like that, Em," he says. "Besides, I am going with Rachel May."

"Oh." Emily reaches out for me and wraps her fingers into my fur, but says nothing more.

"I'm sorry. I didn't realize you thought this was... thought we..."

Emily grimaces and tugs at my fur. She won't even look at Paul as he tries his best to make awkward small talk. He is crazy for choosing mean old Rachel May over Emily, and I'd tell him so if I could. Instead, I focus on being there for Emily as this first crack works its way into her heart.

Eventually Paul gives up on talking and goes back to his home.

Emily and I sit in the garden for another hour before she finally gets up and goes back inside.

Four more years come and go. Paul and Rachel break up almost as quickly as they come together, and Emily moves on to date a much nicer boy named Ethan. He is here with us now, sitting in our backyard garden and scratching the exact right spot near my shoulder. I cannot keep myself from thumping my foot to show Ethan my vast appreciation, no matter how much my joints howl in protest as I make my happy, jerky movements.

"Atta girl, Lulu," he says and gives me a pat on the head before grabbing Emily up into his lap and laying a big kiss on her. I've never seen her as happy as she is with Ethan. He has made my job much easier these past few months, often voicing the sentiments I can only feel, letting Emily know how much we both love her, making sure she is taken care of.

And I know I don't have much time left. My bones have become brittle, and Emily is now a big blur of colors where she was once a defined form. My body has aged even though my spirit doesn't feel any different than it ever has.

Emily knows this too, I think. Sometimes tears form in the corners of her big, beautiful eyes—but she never lets them fall. She's too strong. I've made sure of it. I try to tell her that part of being strong is learning to be vulnerable, but nothing I say translates properly to human language. Besides, she hasn't needed me quite as much since we said goodbye to Jessie and hello to Ethan. My little girl is practically a woman now.

A soft crunching sound drifts through the air, and I am too excited to stay put. Barking furiously, I rush around to the front of the house—just in time to greet the mail carrier on her rounds. This part of the day sits near the top of my list when it comes to the pleasures of being a dog, rivaled only by being able to play and cuddle with Emily, go swimming in our grandparents' lake, and eat delicious steaks.

The mail lady is ready for me. She pulls a small, bacon-flavored treat from the pouch at her waist and tosses it toward me. "How you doing today, Lu?"

Snap! I catch the morsel effortlessly and swallow it in one big bite.

Emily emerges from the side yard. "Anything today?"

"Actually…" The mail lady reaches into her shoulder bag and pulls out a stack of envelopes held together by a thin red rubber band.

"Oh, thank you, thank you, thank you!" Emily plucks the bundle and pulls out the letter on top.

"Have a good one, dear."

Ethan joins us just as Emily has torn into the envelope emblazoned with a fancy seal, and the mail lady has taken her leave. "Is that—?"

"*Shhh*!" Emily scolds, but a smile creeps across her face. Her brows press together, and she mouths the words soundlessly as her eyes scan the page. After a few moments, she refolds the paper and takes a deep breath.

"Did you…?" Ethan's voice trails off, and a worried expression crosses his normally cheerful features.

Emily's eyes dance with a secret, then her head moves up and down. Finally, she screams just as loud as she can, "I got in! I'm going to be a Wolverine!"

"Oh, Emmie. I'm so proud of you!" Ethan grabs her hands, and together they bounce up and down, releasing all their happy energy into the universe.

I jump up and down too. Their excitement is contagious. I don't care that my joints pop and creak beneath my weight. I am just so happy that all of Emily's dreams are now coming true.

The grass outside my window is starting to yellow as the humidity dances through the air in waves and sunbeams filter through the thick glass, chasing away the beginning of a chill. It is almost time.

Emily appears at the bottom of the staircase, a large suitcase pressed into her side. She gives me a pitiful look and says, "I'll be back down soon, Lulu, okay? I just have to pack this one last bag," then bolts up the stairs.

I cannot follow. It is too hard on my brittle hips. Now I spend most days glued to my spot in front of the window. Hip dysplasia, they call it. The beginning of the end for dogs like me.

My eyelids become heavy, and I doze amidst the warmth of a thousand sunny memories.

A soft hand combs through my fur. "C'mon, Lulu, let's go outside." Emily smiles, but it doesn't quite reach her eyes. She stands and helps to pull me up by my armpits.

Together, we pad through the kitchen and out to the garden. It is our spot.

Emily sits on the dried mud and motions for me to join her.

I lay my head in her lap and enjoy the feel of her velvety skin beneath my muzzle.

"You know what happens tomorrow, don't you, girl?" Emily whispers, stroking my fur gently as she speaks. "Ethan and I are leaving for college. I'll be very far away, and I won't be able to see you as much as I'd like."

One tear, then another, escapes down her cheek. "They don't let dogs come, and even though I think it's a silly rule, there's no way to change their minds. Besides, Mom is going to take such great care of you. Dad too."

More tears cascade to the earth and embed themselves among the irises. It's funny how her sorrow will ultimately help something so beautiful to thrive and grow. It is here in the dirt where Jessie was buried, where I will soon be buried too.

And Emily knows. Every word, every touch, every glance tells me so. She hasn't needed me for years now, though she has continued to love me—and I to love her. My purpose was fulfilled a long time ago, yet I've selfishly stuck around for the pure joy of her company, of being able to feel her eyes on me, to know she loved me back.

It has always been I who needed her more. Emily is such a strong young woman, and she is ready for the next phase of life. So too am I.

Emily wipes the tears from her face and rises. "Let's go back inside, Lulu. It's starting to get dark."

But this time I don't obey. Instead, I close my eyes to this life and open them in the next. I hover close to my little girl, but can no longer smell the sweet perfume of our garden nor taste the dampness of the summer air. Still, I can watch. I can stay close to Emily and protect her as we both venture forth into the next chapter of our lives.

Emily raises her head to the sun and smiles. And although it is impossible, I know she understands. Our love for each other is too perfect for even this to keep us apart.

Perhaps it is she who is my angel.

A READER'S GUIDE TO THE PEARL MAKERS UNIVERSE

Welcome to the universe of the Pearl Makers, a special class of angels who guide humanity toward Heaven. To better understand this world, you'll need a few quick definitions first.

Guardian Angels are split into two classes. The **protector angels** are very much in line with what most people think of when they consider guardian angels. Protectors are assigned to a mortal at birth and are to guide them toward **Heaven** through as many births as it takes for them to learn all of life's lessons. The **warden angels** are also guardians, and they too guide their charges toward Heaven. However, a warden's job entails making life for his charge as difficult and rife with hardship as possible. Wardens are assigned to those mortals who commit such terrible deeds that they must be punished in order to make recompense and eventually better their souls.

Only two realms exist within this world, Heaven and Earth. **Hell** is not a place, but rather a condition. Those mortals who are assigned warden angels are put through hell on Earth and must suffer until their souls achieve purity.

Normally, once a soul ascends, it will cross through the **Gates** and enter Heaven, thus becoming a **Pearl**. However, when a warden's charge achieves purity, the charge must then become a warden himself as the final part of his sentence. Only once *his* charge reaches Heaven will he be able to join him.

To achieve their goals, protector angels have two primary powers. The first is **the whisper**, which is the voice of the conscience. The second is **the dodge**, an ability to control movement, which humans often mistake for muscle memory. Warden angels have a third ability: **the pull**. While protectors can only influence their own charges, wardens can influence any mortal soul using this ability as long as their end goal is to effect the suffering of their own charge.

While every individual—angel or mortal—is granted free will, they are also laden with the Plan. **The Plan** entails certain key aspects of life that are an inescapable part of the soul's journey. Questioning the Plan tends only to bring it about faster.

All human life ends, at which point a mortal will either become a Pearl, transform into an angel, or take another birth as a human. There are only two ways for mortals to become angels. The first is by committing acts so unspeakably evil that they must ultimately become a warden to atone for their sins. The second is by performing an act of self-sacrifice, which will turn them into a protector.

If a soul is not qualified to become an angel and is not yet ready to become a Pearl, it is reborn with a new mortal identity—a process commonly referred to as **reincarnation**. Some souls require hundreds of births to reach ascension; rare others only need a few. In extreme cases, some mortals may remember their previous births in a phenomenon known as **past life regression**. This is often caused by protector angels who have a personal connection to their charge and refuse to let go of their own pasts, thus saddling their charges with these whispers of lives that came before.

If you were to ask the Pearl Makers, the meaning of life is simply to experience love in its purest state. Everything comes back to love, knowing it, experiencing it, and giving it to others freely. Once a mortal achieves this, they will be gladly welcomed through the Gates and into Heaven, a place of pure and everlasting love.

ALSO BY MELISSA STORM

THE PEARL MAKERS

Angels in Our Lives

Diving for Pearls

Love Forever, Theo

Shackle My Soul

Angel of Mine

THE CUPID'S BOW SERIES

When I Fall in Love

My Heart Belongs Only to You

I'll Never Stop Loving You

You Make Me Feel So Young

Total Eclipse of the Heart

Tainted Love

I Want to Dance with Somebody

You Belong with Me

She Will Be Loved

Somebody Like You

All I Want for Christmas is You

THE BOOK CELLAR MYSTERIES

Walker Texas Wife

Texas & Tiaras

Remember the Stilettos

Ladies, We Have a Problem

STAND-ALONE NOVELS & NOVELLAS

A Texas Kind of Love

A Cowboy Kind of Love

A Wedding Miracle

Finding Mr. Happily Ever After

A Colorful Life

My Love Will Find You

Melissa also writes Children's Books and Nonfiction as Emlyn Chand. Learn more about those works at www.EmlynChand.com.

About the Author

Melissa Storm is a mother first, and everything else second. She used to write under a pseudonym, but finally had the confidence to come out as herself to the world. Her fiction is highly personal and often based on true stories. Writing is Melissa's way of showing her daughter just how beautiful life can be, when you pay attention to the everyday wonders that surround us.

Melissa loves books so much, she married fellow author Falcon Storm. Between the two of them, there are always plenty of imaginative, awe-inspiring stories to share. Melissa and Falcon also run the business Novel Publicity together, where she works as publisher, marketer, editor, and all-around business mogul. When she's not reading, writing, or child-rearing, Melissa spends time relaxing at home in the company of her three dogs and five parrots. She never misses an episode of *The Bachelor* or her nightly lavender-infused soak in the tub. Ahh, the simple luxuries that make life worth living.

Melissa loves hearing from readers.

Please feel free to reach out!

www.MelStorm.com

Made in the USA
Charleston, SC
30 November 2016